A Duchess for Thorneshire Manor

A Clean Regency Romance Novel

Martha Barwood

Copyright © 2024 by Martha Barwood
All Rights Reserved.
This book may not be reproduced or transmitted in any form without the written permission of the publisher. In no way is it legal to reproduce, duplicate, or transmit, any part of this document in either electronic means or in printed format. Recording of this publication is strictly prohibited and any storage of this document is not allowed unless with written permission from the publisher.

Table of Contents

Prologue..3
Chapter One..6
Chapter Two 15
Chapter Three..23
Chapter Four..31
Chapter Five...39
Chapter Six...50
Chapter Seven..57
Chapter Eight 66
Chapter Nine..72
Chapter Ten 78
Chapter Eleven..85
Chapter Twelve...90
Chapter Thirteen..95
Chapter Fourteen 102
Chapter Fifteen...111
Chapter Sixteen 119
Chapter Seventeen 127
Chapter Eighteen 132
Chapter Nineteen 138
Chapter Twenty 142
Chapter Twenty-One 146
Chapter Twenty-Two 150
Chapter Twenty-Three..155
Chapter Twenty-Four..164
Epilogue 171
Extended Epilogue 177

Prologue

The Thorneshire Estate, 1806

His cheeks hurt.

It struck Calum suddenly, the realization that he had never smiled this hard in his nine-and-twenty years on earth. This level of happiness, this zest for his future. He'd meandered through his days lazily, happy only to be able to open his eyes each morning. There was never anything that gave him true, unending pleasure.

Now, the subject of all his happiness stood across the room bearing a smile just as broad.

Calum could not hear what was being said. He only saw her, his eyes tracing the outline of her face as if he hadn't spent the past year committing her to his memory. He could close his eyes and imagine the gentle curve of her cheeks, her upturned nose, the exact hue of her honey-blond hair currently styled in those lovely curls he adored on her. Calum had a lifetime ahead of him to admire every inch of her, watching her change throughout the years they would spend together. He intended to start right now.

He couldn't believe that Lady Violet Henderson was now his wife.

"Wouldn't you say, Your Grace?"

"Certainly," Calum murmured absently. He didn't know who he was talking to or what about. He didn't care. He watched as Violet tilted her head to the side and nodded to whatever her friend was saying to her. But her eyes trailed as well, as if she could not focus either. Eventually, they landed on Calum and her smile widened.

Calum straightened. After a year of courtship, his heart still skipped a beat when she looked at him. Her eyes narrowed a little with that mischievous glint that always excited him. It took everything in him not to leap out of his chair and go to her side.

They would have plenty of time together later, after all. Tomorrow, after the wedding breakfast was over, they would be heading to Scotland for their honeymoon. Alone with each other, they would have all the time in the world for private smiles and loving embraces.

Violet turned slightly to face him and suddenly, no one else existed. Calum ran his hand down his face, shifting in his chair as he watched her slowly lift her glass of wine to her lips. She always knew how to taunt him.

This wedding breakfast could not be over quickly enough.

With a wink, Violet turned her attention back to her friend and Calum tried to do the same today. He realized with a start that it was Stephen by his side, his cousin and estate steward, who did not seem to notice Calum's absent-mindedness. He focused once more on the conversation and tried to keep his eyes off his wife. Which was easier said than done.

Calum counted the seconds, the minutes, the hours until they were finally alone. At last, the wedding breakfast came to an end. By that time, the sun was slowly giving way to darkness as evening came upon them. Violet went upstairs to change out of her wedding dress while Calum remained in the parlor with his third glass of wine in his hand.

That was when he heard the scream.

At first, he froze, unable to come to terms with what he'd heard. Then realization sank like cold stones in the pit of his stomach. He dropped his wine, hardly hearing the crash of glass as he raced out of the room.

Hallways flew past him in a blur. He didn't think it possible for him to move so fast but, within what felt like seconds, he burst through the door of their bedchamber. Calum swallowed past the lump in his throat, his heart hammering.

Violet lay lifelessly on the bed.

"What happened?" He heard the words come from his lips even though he didn't realize that he'd spoken. His limbs seemed to turn to mush as he made his way to her side. "What happened to her?"

"I don't know, Your Grace." Mrs. Dawson, the housekeeper, sounded as distraught as he felt. He could hear the tears in her voice. She shifted out of his way but she kept her hands in Violet's legs, shaking her gently. "I stepped out of the room for a second and when I returned…"

"The physician." Calum's voice was raw, hardly audible. But she nodded as if she knew exactly what he wanted.

"Yes, Your Grace." In a flash, Mrs. Dawson was out the door, leaving him alone with his wife's lifeless body.

She was ashen. Her beautiful lips were white, her body cold to the touch. Calum pulled her into his arms, blinking away the tears that blurred his vision. The truth of the situation settled in the back of his mind but he refused to acknowledge it. He would wait. He wouldn't dare to acknowledge the possibility.

Calum didn't know how long he spent there with her in his arms but all of a sudden, the room was full. Mrs. Dawson and Stephen were there, and Dr. Percival Marsh was gently taking Violet from his arms. Calum made a groan of protest but he knew he couldn't do anything. Stephen was already by his side, pulling him out of the room.

"He needs space and time, Calum," Stephen was saying. "She will be all right."

Calum shook his head and wiped his tears. He didn't dare to acknowledge the truth lingering in the back of his head but it settled in his heart.

By the time the physician emerged from the bedchamber, Calum took one look at his face and the fragile pieces left of his heart crumbled into dust.

Chapter One

Thorneshire Estate, London Countryside, 1811

She stared at him with betrayal in her eyes. That was the first thing he noticed. Not the blood running from her eyes, staining her cheeks and lips red. Not the way she shivered, her wet hair plastered to her neck as if she had been dunked into a pool of water. Not the manner in which her hands flexed at her sides—open and close, open and close, open and close.

It was the raw pain of hurt that shone in those once-beautiful eyes that tore him to shreds.

"You did this," Violet said. "You did not save me."

"I tried to." His words would not reach her. Even as they echoed around him, he could tell she heard nothing.

Her hands closed again. She was in her nightgown, he realized suddenly, the same thing she had been in when she'd passed away. And they were...they were in that room again.

"You should have been there," she said softly. Not soft enough though to keep from slicing through him. "You should have stopped this from happening."

"Violet—"

"No!" Her screech sent him careening to the other side of the room.

"Violet, please!"

"You should have helped me!" she wailed. "You should have—"

Calum shot upright, heaving. Sweat clung to his skin, his heart racing. Another night enduring the same dream. This time, it had taken every strength he possessed to force himself out of it.

Her presence lingered though, as it always did. Night after night, she visited him. And each time, he either suffered through the guilt and pain or forced himself awake when it became too much. Either way, his days were destined to be long and lonesome.

He raked his fingers through his damp hair, trying to calm his breathing. At least he'd slept through the night this time. Most times, he woke in the middle of the night with no hope of resting again. Sunlight peaked through his heavy drapes and the sight was enough to darken his mood. If he had any strength he would pull the drapes fully closed and stew in the darkness.

Violet's pained eyes flashed in his mind again. Calum pulled himself out of the bed, staggering over to the chamber pot. Every step he took filled him with the familiar wave of anger.

Violet was right. He should have been there. If he had been fast enough, if only he hadn't allowed her to leave his side, she would still be here. It was his fault.

With a roar of frustration, he picked up the chamber pot and threw it across the room. The resounding crash gave him a small bit of satisfaction, it wasn't enough though to distract him from the gaping hole in the middle of his chest.

The door burst open and a stocky man with graying hair raced in, panting. His valet, never too far at this hour of the day, looked terrified. "Your Grace? Your Grace!"

"Stop the shouting," Calum grumbled. "I'm right here."

Relief and worry washed over the valet's face the moment he spotted Calum standing near the far corner of the room. He took a tentative step in Calum's direction. "Are you all right, Your Grace? I heard a loud crash and—"

"I am fine." He stared at the mess he'd caused at the other end of the room. "Leave me be."

"But, Your Grace—"

"I said, leave me be!" Calum roared. He whirled on the man, feeling another bite of satisfaction when the concern on his face melted into true fear. "I have no patience for your pity nor do I wish to be in the presence of a bumbling man who can hardly get his words out! Do not let me repeat myself!"

His valet nodded hastily and scrambled out of the room, leaving Calum alone again. Just the way he liked it. He didn't need anyone's empathy when he could hardly muster up any for himself. If he could spend his days alone in his manor, lurking in the darkness with nothing but whiskey as company, it would be a fitting punishment.

But the Duke of Thorneshire had duties. Duties he was content to ignore until they became pressing.

He dressed alone, dragging himself through the motions. He had little urge to leave his chambers but being here only brought back memories of that day with a vengeance. So the next best thing would be to drink his sorrows away until he could remember nothing at all.

Without his valet's help, it took him nearly an hour to don suitable clothing for the day. By the time he was ready to leave his chambers, none of his anger had abated. He marched down the hallway, heading in the direction of his study where he could lock himself away without a soul to bother him.

He had no such luck. The first soul that happened upon him came in the form of kind eyes and homely features.

"Good morning, Your Grace," Mrs. Dawson greeted with a slight curtsy.

Calum forced his scowl into submission. Something about the way she looked at him made him think he didn't do a very good job. "Good morning, Mrs. Dawson."

"How did you sleep?" she asked like she always did. Every day for the past five years now.

"Good," he responded, like he always would even though they both knew that he was lying.

They delved into brief seconds of silence that spoke far too loudly. Calum knew what Mrs. Dawson was thinking. She'd been the manor's housekeeper since he was an infant and understood him far better than he would like. He didn't have to say that he was still in mourning. And she didn't have to say that she prayed day and night for him to be better one day. He didn't like the pity in her eyes any more than he liked it in anyone else's, but Mrs. Dawson was the only servant in the manor he wouldn't dare shout at.

After a long while, she said, "Your breakfast is ready in your study, Your Grace. Should I open the drapes?"

"No." He stalked by her and she fell in step with him, just slightly behind. Calum gritted his teeth.

"It is a lovely morning," she insisted. "Perhaps it shall brighten your mood."

Calum stopped to look at her, barely holding back his scowl.

"Or perhaps it shall not," she said calmly. She clasped her hands in front of her. "I hope you enjoy your meal and your morning nonetheless."

They both knew that was impossible. Calum hadn't enjoyed a single thing since the day Violet died.

But his only response was a curt nod before continuing on his way, grateful that she didn't continue to follow him. He hoped to continue his usual practice of wallowing in his pain alone. Later in the morning, Stephen would find him, he knew. And Calum would have to pretend to listen to everything his cousin said even though they both knew that Stephen would be taking care of his ducal matters anyhow.

For now, he was alone.

For now, he could honor Violet's memory by refusing to live.

The food tasted like ash but Calum barreled through it since it had been a day since he'd eaten a proper meal. His hands moved without thinking, falling back into his old practice of eating anything put in front of him. While his mind and heart lacked an appetite for food, his body still yearned for it.

He finished it quickly and was already heading to the sideboard to pour himself his first glass of whiskey, even though it was still morning. The proper hours to drink did not matter to him any longer.

"Your Grace?' Without waiting for a response, the door opened and his butler stepped in.

"What do you want?" Calum snapped, annoyed.

Unlike the other servants, his butler had mastered the art of hiding his expressions. But Calum knew he feared him. "You have a visitor, Your Grace."

"Are you out of your mind? I am in no mood for company. Send them away."

"I told them, Your Grace, but..." He trailed off, a look of uncertainty cracking his usually placid expression.

Calum glowered at him. "But what?"

"But he knows better than to send me away, that's what." A petite lady breezed past the threshold, stopping in the center of the study. She gave Calum a broad smile. "How lovely to see you up, my dear. Have you had breakfast yet?"

Calum sighed. His godmother, Lady Eleanor Gardner of Yulebridge, was not someone his butler could simply send away. Calum could only imagine how terrible such a conversation would go.

He waved a hand, silently sending his butler away. Then he poured himself his drink, knowing that he would need it in order to get through the conversation he was about to have.

"Why are you here, Eleanor?" he asked wearily.

Eleanor regarded him calmly, saying nothing about the drink in his hand, though he knew she wanted to. She waited until he sank into the chair behind his desk before saying, "I came to check on you. It has been a while, hasn't it?"

"I suppose." He hardly paid attention to the passage of time any longer. The days blended together endlessly.

"A week, I believe," she went on. She began to walk back and forth, her hands folded in front of her. Though a widow and sister to his late father, Eleanor looked half her age, with dark hair barely touched with gray and a nearly wrinkle free face. "It has been so long that I nearly forgot that you are a paramour of liquor."

Calum regarded his aunt with thinly veiled annoyance. He was in no mood for her dramatics today. "Is there a reason you've paid me a visit so early?"

"Yes," she answered simply. "But can't I ask you how you are feeling first?"

"Right now? I am a bit irritated."

"That is a pity." Her bottom lip popped out in a pout. "I believe what I am about to say will only irritate you further."

Calum braced himself. That didn't sound good.

She continued to walk back and forth in silence. Calum watched her, sipping his whiskey as he tried to wait it out.

At last, she said, "Very well, I shall simply be direct and speak my mind. I have come to invite you to attend my annual spring ball next week."

"No."

His response came so quickly that she started, blinking at him. "Perhaps you should give it a bit of thought before you answer, Calum."

"There is no need to. I cannot think of anything I would hate more than to attend a ball."

"It is not as bad as you think," she insisted. She finally sat in one of the armchairs facing the desk, looking distressed. "You once enjoyed them, if you can recall."

There were many things Calum once enjoyed. Now he hardly tolerated opening his eyes in the mornings. "I will not be attending the ball, Eleanor."

"Well, I will not be taking no for an answer," she insisted.

"Need I remind you that you are the Duke of Thorneshire? You have duties to fulfill and right now, the most important duty is securing the dukedom by producing an heir."

"An heir?" Calum echoed, incredulous. How could she suggest such a thing after what happened five years ago?

She nodded, lips pulled into a tight line of determination. "Yes, an heir." Then she reached across the table to touch his hand gently. "I understand your pain, Calum. I do. Losing someone you love so suddenly takes something from you than cannot easily be recovered."

Calum said nothing, fighting the urge to tell her that no one could possibly understand him. He'd been there when Eleanor's husband died. Since she'd been quite young when she married, and her husband had been a wealthy but elderly viscount, one would think she would be relieved when he finally passed. But Calum knew Eleanor had grown to love her late husband. And the loss of his absence was void not easily filled.

But he died peacefully in his sleep, at an age that would be deemed easy to accept by those who loved him. Violet had been young. They'd just begun their life together. One minute she was there and the next she was gone.

Calum didn't need to say the words, he realized, because Eleanor looked at him as if she knew what he did not speak aloud. Even so, she continued, "Your father would want you to carry on your name, Calum. The Hawthorn legacy and the Thorneshire dukedom cannot end with you."

She just knew to strike him where it hurt. Calum avoided her eyes, finishing the rest of his drink. "It's too soon," he pushed out.

"It's been five years," she countered. "If left to yourself, you will mourn her forever."

"There is nothing wrong with that," he snapped without thinking.

Eleanor didn't draw back. Instead, she curled her fingers around his, eyes softening. "I don't want you to lose who you are by the end of it, Calum. You must remember your duties. And perhaps finding someone to share your company may bring some sunlight to your dark days."

That he sincerely doubted. There was no brightening his days. He was destined to mourn Violet for as long as he lived, giving up pieces of himself if that was what it took to atone for his sins.

But he didn't dare to voice such morose thoughts to his aunt. He knew she worried about him enough already.

"Just attend the ball," she urged again. "That is all I ask. And then we can take it from there."

Calum heaved a sigh. She was right. Even though he hated to admit it, he would be doing a disservice to his late father if he let their name die with him. The duties he had been running from all this time were finally catching up to him.

"Just the ball then," he conceded at last.

Eleanor's face lit up with pleasure. "Marvelous! You shall not regret it, I assure you."

Calum sincerely doubted that. He said nothing though as he stood to get his next drink. This time, he brought the decanter back to the desk, ignoring Eleanor's look of disapproval.

Even though she'd succeeded in what she had come here to do, Eleanor did not seem to be in any urgency to leave. Calum sat back and listened as she talked about trivial nonsense like conversations she'd had with her friends or upcoming events she was excited about. He knew what she was trying to do—filling the emptiness with lively chatter. Perhaps she hoped that he would not feel too lonely. Calum left her be and at one point, he fell so deeply into his thoughts that he hardly heard a word she said.

After a while, there was a knock on the door. "Calum?" came Stephen's low baritone.

"Oh, Stephen, come!" Eleanor responded before Calum got the chance.

Stephen slipped into the room bearing the account books in one hand. He pushed his spectacles up his nose, looking mildly surprised at Eleanor's presence. "Aunt Eleanor, I am surprised to see you here."

"Yes, well, I had something important to speak with Calum about," she explained, rising. "But I shall take my leave now. I see that you two are about to talk about more important things than my silly gossip."

It occurred to Calum that he should walk her to the front door. It was the gentlemanly thing to do, the way he was raised by his upright parents. But he stayed seated, like the heavy hand of lingering sorrow was keeping him in his seat.

Eleanor flashed Calum a smile that was laced with her own sorrow. He could only imagine how difficult it was for her to see him this way, but he didn't allow himself to linger on it. This was who he was now. A shell of his former self without Violet.

Stephen straightened as Eleanor drew closer. "Allow me to—"

"Don't you worry," she said, laying a hand on his chest as she went by. "I am confident in my ability to navigate my way out. Don't forget I have been wandering these hallways far before you boys were born."

Stephen was polite enough to offer up a laugh for that. Calum was not. Thankfully, his aunt did not stay any longer, leaving him alone with his cousin.

He sighed heavily. He supposed his lonely morning was not going to be as lonely as he hoped.

Stephen turned to him and Calum didn't have to look at his face to know he wore a quizzical expression. "What was that about?"

Calum heaved another sigh. "Eleanor thought it fit to invite me to her upcoming spring ball."

"Ball?" Stephen sounded incredulous. He drew nearer, sinking into the same armchair Eleanor had just vacated. "Why would she do that?"

"She believes that it is time for me to bear an heir." Saying it aloud sounded like a betrayal. How could he even think about tying himself to another lady?

"Hm." Stephen said nothing and they lapsed into silence as he laid out the account books. Calum ignored him. He knew what that sound meant. Either he disapproved of the idea or was waiting for the right moment to voice his opinion. He hoped it was the former—that way, Stephen would keep it to himself.

So Calum felt a bite of surprise when Stephen said, "I do not think that is a good idea."

Calum frowned a little. "You do not?"

Stephen shook his head, pushing his spectacles back up his nose. Calum couldn't understand why he didn't buy a smaller pair since those were clearly too big. Or had his face just gotten slimmer? Stephen had always been quite lanky with slim features, from the slant of his nose to the jut of his chin to his bony limbs.

"Allow me to be precise," Stephen said, which was odd since he was nothing but precise. "What I mean to say is that such a thing makes me a bit trepidant. Reemerging in society amongst the gossip that spreads like wildfire about you may only harm your reputation further rather than aid it."

Calum's frown only deepened at that. "Not that it matters to me but I do not care about my reputation. You know that."

"I know." Stephen regarded him evenly. "But such gossip hinges on your late wife's name. Whispers will begin once more regarding her mysterious death."

"There was nothing mysterious about it," Calum pushed through gritted teeth. This conversation was quickly going into territory that he could not handle. "She died of natural causes", he said, even though in his mind he could feel that the cause of her death was inexplicable.

"I know that," Stephen stated calmly. "But the ton cares not about the truth. Only about what sounds more interesting."

"Enough," Calum snapped. "I do not want to talk about this."

"Very well. But consider my words, cousin. I only speak in your best interest."

Calum didn't grace that with a response and Stephen didn't seem to care about receiving one. Ever the diligent one, he began the task of reviewing the account books, clearly unperturbed by Calum's lack of interest in what he was doing. Calum would not have been able to participate even if he wanted to. Not when the only thing he could think about was Violet. Her memory, her death. They warred together in his head, driving him to drink more.

They were both right. Deep down, he knew it. If he dared to step out into society, rumors will rise once more about how his wife died. If he continued to hide away in his manor, he may lose the chance to bear an heir and pass on his name.

Calum finished his drink and poured himself another. All of a sudden, the full decanter of whiskey didn't seem nearly enough.

Chapter Two

The dress was three years old and hopelessly out of fashion. Clarissa smoothed her hand down the front of it, narrowing her eyes at any suspicious area that might need mending. She didn't like it. It was too small for her now, the color did not complement her complexion, and worse of all, it was old-fashioned. But it was one of the only dresses she had left.

Slowly, she raised her eyes to her face. And sighed. She missed her earrings. She missed wearing that small locket around her neck no matter what time of day it was. She missed the lovely headdresses she would don on special days, sitting prettily between her silky, dark brown hair. There were so many things about her old life that she wanted back. Things she would never get again.

For one, she was no longer in her own bedchamber. Clarissa couldn't even remember how it looked. It had been two years since she'd left their London townhouse to stay with her aunt and uncle and the lovely bedchamber they had put her in looked nothing like her own. She was yet to make it her own, as empty of character as she felt.

She didn't sigh. She was tired of sighing. It had been two years so this was her life now. It was about time she got used to it.

Clarissa ran her fingers through her hair in an idle manner as she turned and left her room. She hadn't bothered to style it the way she usually did. Rather than intricate curls, she twisted the top of her hair into a chignon while the rest tumbled down her back. It comforted her to touch her hair, the only thing that remained truly hers.

"You look lovely, Clarissa!"

Clarissa came to a halt, smiling at her sister emerging from her own chambers. Again she was struck by how mature Louisa looked, now at ten-and-five years old. It was like looking at her younger self. Louisa was still so full of life that it was hard to believe she'd been there when their lives had been turned upside down two years ago. She endured everything with a smile while Clarissa constantly remained in the past.

"As do you, Louisa," Clarissa said, slipping her arm through hers. Even though Louisa's dress was also out of fashion, it fit her far better. She'd styled her hair, the same dark brown as Clarissa's though much shorter. "And I see that you are in a good mood."

"Because it is a lovely day," Louisa chirped. "Can you blame me?"

Clarissa's laugh came easily, surprisingly so. "No, I suppose I cannot. Then I take it you intend on spending it outdoors?"

Louisa pouted in thought. Together, they turned and continued along their way down the hallway. "I am not sure. Do you think Uncle will be willing to let me go horse riding today?"

"I do not see why not," Clarissa said honestly. "Uncle falls prey to your charm like everyone else. If you ask, I doubt that he will deny you."

Louisa laughed, the sound instantly lifting her spirits. If she let her mind wander too far, she would begin to wonder when Louisa would lose her spark, if she would become as fearful of the future as Clarissa was. But she didn't dare let that train of thought take hold. As the eldest, Clarissa would do anything to save her sister from worrying about a single thing.

"Let us see then, shall we?" Louisa said, a spark of challenge in her eyes.

They made it down to the drawing room and the moment they walked through the door, Clarissa's mood plummeted to the floor. Her mother sat in her usual spot by the window, gazing out with that blank look on her face. She looked hastily dressed, as if she had barely given much thought into what she was wearing. Her hair seemed unbrushed. And she sat so still that Clarissa was almost afraid to draw closer, lest she startled her.

The Dowager Baroness of Quelshire had once been a proud woman. Her shell sat there now, nothing but a husk without a soul. After everything that happened two years ago, Lady Olivia Wyndham fell into a deep melancholy and never recovered.

"Good morning, Mother!" Louisa chirped, letting go of Clarissa's arm to flock to their mother's side.

Clarissa warily drew nearer, sitting next to Louisa. She studied Olivia's face, searching for signs of life like she usually did. And as usual, disappointment came swiftly when she saw nothing shining back at her.

Louisa barreled on, as if unperturbed by her mother's state.

"Don't you think it is a lovely day? I have not gone horse-riding in quite some time so I am hoping to ask Uncle if he will allow me to have one of the horses for the afternoon."

Olivia did not answer. Clarissa couldn't remember the last time Olivia spoke. The shock of her husband's death and the state he had left them in seemed to have settled far too deeply in her mind and she was yet to recover.

A part of Clarissa couldn't blame her. She'd only been ten-and-nine when the Baron of Quelshire passed away. The death of her father had been sad enough, but the trauma that came with learning of his horrible financial decisions nearly broke her. In a matter of a month, their comfortable life had been turned upside down. Debt was far too simple a word for the destitution they'd found themselves in. And with it came such a horrible mark on their reputation as a family that Clarissa had lost all hope of finding a husband.

Clarissa had lost more than one parent in the span of a month. And with it came the constantly distressing worry about how they would survive. Their lacking reputation and no dowry meant the chances of Louisa and her getting married were slim. And she did not want to be dependent on her aunt and uncle for any longer than was necessary, though she saw no way out of it right now.

Louisa chattered on. Clarissa bit her tongue, wanting to tell Louisa to stop. But the sound of her voice was comforting. If she tried hard enough, Clarissa could pretend that nothing bad had happened at all.

Before long, two maids entered the room bearing trays, cutlery, and pots of tea. Behind them was Lord Robert Miller, the Earl of Santbury and his wife, Martha. Robert's eyes instantly fell on Olivia. As her older brother, Clarissa could only imagine how distressing it had to be for him to see his younger sister in such a state.

"Good morning, Uncle!" Louisa chirped. "Good morning, Aunt."

"Louisa, darling, you seem to be in a lovely mood," Martha observed as she came to sit with them. "It makes me wonder if you know of our news already."

"News?" Clarissa spoke up, frowning.

Robert claimed the spot next to his wife. He rested a hand on her rotund belly, clearly without thought. They were a lovely couple, Clarissa thought again. Though he was far older than Olivia, he'd married much later. Now, after four years of trying, Martha was finally with child.

"Goodness, Martha," he said lovingly. "And here I thought you wanted to create suspense before telling them."

"I cannot help myself," Martha giggled. She leaned into her husband's loving touch and Clarissa had to fight the pang of envy at the sight. "I am so excited that I can hardly contain it."

"Excited about what?" Louisa asked. "What are you talking about?"

The earl and countess exchanged looks. Clarissa squirmed uncertainly. What if they intended to put them out? They had been dependent on Robert and Martha for almost two years now, contributing very little to their household. And at her age of one-and-twenty, with no wealth at all, she had no hopes of marrying. Were they going to tell them to leave to fend for themselves?

She'd been dreading this moment. Even though their happy smiles told her that perhaps her pessimistic thoughts were only that, Clarissa knew that it was only a matter of time before her uncle grew tired of their presence. Family or no, they were burdens. Her mother was like a raggedy, lifeless doll. Her sister was far too young to be of any help to anyone. And Clarissa was quickly nearing spinsterhood with no suitable matches. They were doomed.

No one noticed her guard building up around her as Robert said, "I have decided to fund a dowry for Clarissa to attend the upcoming season."

"I understand," Clarissa began. She swallowed past the lump in her throat, her gaze fixed on her lap in the hopes that no one would see her tears. "We shall begin packing our things."

"Clarissa, didn't you hear?" Louisa nudged her excitedly. "Uncle said he would fund your dowry! You will be attending the Season!"

"Yes, I heard—" She broke off, looking sharply at her sister. "I am what?"

Martha's laughter drew Clarissa's attention. "I told you that she would be too stunned to speak. Oh just thinking about it brings me back to when I debuted at my first Season. I can only imagine how excited you are, Clarissa"

Excited? No, not at all. Stunned and in a debilitating state of disbelief. Quite so.

"I don't understand," she managed to say. "Why would you do such a thing?"

"Why wouldn't I?" Robert countered as if the answer was obvious. "You are my niece. And after all that has happened to you, I think it rather sad that you are unable to step into society the way you should have by now. If I remember correctly, you were to debut before Edward passed, correct?"

Clarissa could only manage a nod. Louisa was buzzing with elation next to her.

"And once you found out the truth of his management, you were unable to." Robert shook his head as if he was sincerely saddened by the thought. "Business has been going quite well as of late so it will not harm us to contribute to your launch into society. It is about time you marry, don't you think?"

Clarissa didn't know what to say. Her mind was a whirlwind, uncertainty and hope warring in her heart. Thankfully, Louisa easily filled the silence.

"How exciting!" she gushed. "I've always wanted to attend balls during the Season. What about Clarissa's wardrobe? Surely she shouldn't attend a single event in such old-fashioned garments."

"I am grateful to be attending at all," Clarissa said quickly, shooting her sister a warning glance.

Martha laughed again. "Not to worry. I shall oversee the improvement of all your wardrobes. Yours as well, Olivia."

There was a brief moment of silence as they waited for Olivia to acknowledge what was being said. Of course, she said nothing, hardly moving.

Robert went on as if they hadn't paused at all. "And, to make this news even more exciting, we have already received our first invitation to a ball."

"Oh, tell us!" Louisa squealed. Clarissa found herself leaning over slightly in anticipation.

"The Dowager Viscountess of Yulebridge will be hosting her spring ball in the coming week and wishes for all to be in attendance. Which means there is quite a lot of preparation to be done before then. I hope you two are ready."

"We are," Clarissa and Louisa said in unison, Louisa in her usual excitable manner and Clarissa with firm determination. Her own enthusiasm lingered underneath the trepidation she felt at this sudden turn of events. After losing hope of their future, slowly beginning to believe that their ruined reputation would be the end of them, she was being given another chance.

And she couldn't squander it. She would take this opportunity by the horns and emerge at the other end in a secured marriage. One where she could take care of her mother and sister and secure Louisa's own future one day.

"Marry?"

All eyes turned to Olivia. Stunned silence settled around them.

Olivia's eyes fluttered and Clarissa realized she had not been mistaken. Her mother had spoken. "You will marry?" Olivia whispered. Painstakingly slow, she turned and locked eyes with Clarissa. Something shadowed her expression, the sight of it making Clarissa's tongue grow thick in her mouth.

Before anyone could attempt to respond, Olivia's eyes rolled to the back of her head. Robert caught her before she could hit the ground.

"Quickly, call the butler!" he barked to no one in particular but Louisa was already on her feet, rushing out the door. Clarissa didn't know what Martha did. Her attention was on her mother, already sinking to her knees to come face to face with her.

"Mother," she called desperately, patting her cheek. She swallowed the bile of fear that rushed up her throat, realizing that her mother's face was hot to the touch. As hot as her father's had been days before his death. "Mother, open your eyes, please."

That day came rushing back to her. It was her father laying limp before her instead, breathing so heavily that she had been afraid to touch him. Fear tore at her insides as she tried her best to remain calm, as she tried not to think that she might be losing another parent all over again.

And then the door opened and the butler came rushing in with Louisa on his heels. He sank to Olivia's side, popping open a bottle of smelling salt and putting it under her chin. They all waited with bated breaths for her to stir.

At least she did. It began as another flutter of her eyelids and Louisa let out a sob. Clarissa put her hand over her mouth, holding back her own silent cries of relief when her mother's eyes opened.

"Bring her up to her room," Robert ordered, even though he didn't have to. Clarissa was already moving to her mother's side, guiding her to a stand. Louisa quickly claimed her other side and, together, they helped her out of the room with the butler trailing behind, smelling salt still in hand.

As they went on, Olivia seemed to regain more of her consciousness. She hardly helped herself walk, dragging herself along and weighing them down. Clarissa didn't complain though. It had been so long since she'd heard her mother speak that she couldn't help the sparkle of hope that her health was beginning to improve. Right now she could handle a little dead weight if it meant that her mother's mind might be returning.

"Lay her down gently," Clarissa said softly upon reaching Olivia's room. With Louisa's help, they laid her on the bed. Olivia immediately curled onto her side, tucked her arm under her head, and stared at the wall.

The butler returned to his duties shortly after, but not before leaving the bottle of smelling salts by her bedside. After a moment, Louisa did as well, claiming that she needed a bit of sunshine and fresh air. Clarissa stood there for far too long, staring down at her mother and wondering when things would begin to feel normal again.

The last time she'd felt anything close to normalcy had been a façade designed by her father. They'd been living a false life without knowing it—every frivolous purchase they made, every platter of food on their table, only making things worse. And with her mother in the state she was in now, the responsibility rested on Clarissa to save her family. A responsibility that did nothing but distress her every day since she hadn't a clue how to go about it.

Now she was being given a chance. She would not let it slip through her fingers.

After a long while, she left her mother alone and went to the only room that brought her solace—the library. Clarissa quickly found the writing desk tucked between two bookshelves in the corner of the room and pulled free clean sheets of paper.

Her poems were the only thing of the past she had, the only way of expressing the deep waves of conflicting emotions that plagued her day by day. She could spend hours writing, pouring her heart into the words that would never be seen by another soul. Some day were more despondent than others. But her poetry today sang a different tune.

They spoke of hope and longing, and a perfect night at Lady Yulebridge's ball.

Chapter Three

This was a terrible mistake. No matter how many times he recognized that fact, Calum remained where he was. Even as reluctance mounted in him by the second, he stayed seated and tried not to bolt from the room.

He was in his aunt's guest bedchamber, having spent the night there after her desperate pleas. He'd given in only because he'd held out hope that perhaps being away from Thorneshire estate might bring him a night of dreamless sleep.

He had no such luck.

In fact, his nightmares plagued him more fiercely than usual. No matter how hard he tried, he was bound to them, watching his wife die over and over again, each time more traumatizing than the last. He had awoken a few hours before dawn drenched in sweat, with a terrible megrim and a foul mood.

Eleanor had stayed out of his way for most of the morning but she didn't miss her chance to remind him of his promise to attend the ball this evening. Not a day went by without her reminding him of it, as if applying more pressure would only ensure that he attended. Calum hated to admit that she was right. Eleanor was capable of inciting strains of guilt he'd never felt before and, before he knew what was happening, he was agreeing to things he hadn't given a second thought to.

Like shaving before the ball. The ball was set to commence in less than an hour and he was stuck in this chair while his bumbling valet carefully carved away the thick bush of hair he'd boasted for years now.

Suddenly, Calum felt a sharp sting of pain. He sucked in a breath and his valet pounced away.

"F-forgive me, Your Grace," he stammered, bowing his head. "It was an accident. My h-hand is shaking and—"

"Get out, you doddering fool!" Calum barked, grabbing the towel nearby to press against his cheek. The other man blanched but wasted no time in doing as he was told.

Calum leaped out of the chair, marching to the mirror that sat on his dresser. Upon inspection, the cut was not deep. In fact, it was hardly noticeable. Staunching the flow of blood had saved it, he assumed.

But that didn't help his mood. If anything, it only worsened it. That was proof, if any, that he should not go anywhere this evening.

He braced his hands on the dresser, taking in deep breaths to calm himself. It did nothing. He wanted to leave this place and send a letter later to his aunt explaining his absence. She would be quite upset with him but surely that was better than enduring what was to come. He could already picture the ballroom being filled with guests, faceless and aimless people who did nothing but talk about the lives of others. A waste of his time.

I'll just leave, he thought, turning to the door. *Eleanor will not realise that I am gone until it is too late.*

Even as the thought crossed his mind he knew that he was wrong. Eleanor would be waiting for his arrival. He wouldn't be surprised if she even posted her footmen around the perimeter of her manor to watch out for him leaving the premises.

Calum drew in a long breath, tossing the towel aside. Perhaps he could sneak to the parlor and have himself a few glasses of liquor before he had to endure the night. The thought was tempting enough to lure him to the door, but then he turned away at the last second. Attending the ball would certainly be easier if he was a little in his cups but he didn't feel like risking Eleanor's wrath if she were to take notice of it.

So he waited. Stewed in his silence. Finished shaving his face carefully. And fought the urge to return to his manor and lament in the quiet of his study like he usually did.

By the time the ball began, Calum was too hesitant to attend. He waited another hour before he finally left the guest chambers and made his way down to the ballroom. The closer he drew, the louder the sound of a pianoforte playing within became. He lingered out in the hallway for a few seconds, watching as more guests were escorted inside.

God help me.

He was many things. But a coward was not one of them. So he plunged into ballroom, ignoring the eyes that were instantly drawn to him. He spotted his aunt immediately, standing near the door greeting those who entered. She was so engaged in conversation with another lady that she didn't spot him right away.

Calum quickly ducked towards the furthest wall away from her, intending to remain out of her sight as long as he possibly could. She could only try dragging him around with her if he wasn't careful.

Eyes followed him as he went by. Calum tried to ignore them but the whispers were not so easy. They rose like a wave and he heard bits and pieces. His name, Violet's, her death. He hadn't even been here long and the old rumors were already being revived.

He knew what they said about him, knew that his unsavory reputation led others to believe that he had been responsible for Violet's death. Calum didn't care about those rumors. He'd spent the past five years blaming himself for what happened so hearing others do the same did not affect him in the slightest.

It was the attention he didn't like. It was knowing that it was only a matter of time before someone approached him.

"Calum!"

Calum froze at his aunt's voice. He didn't dare turn but she moved quickly, slipping in front of him before he could pretend he did not hear her and escape. She caught his arm as if she knew what he intended to do.

"My, you look lovely!" she gushed. "It has been so long since I have seen your face properly."

"Take a good look, Eleanor," he couldn't help but grumble. "Because I shan't be doing it again."

Eleanor shook her head disapprovingly. "You are very handsome, Calum, with or without the beard. But you know as well as I that a clean-shaven appearance is far more appealing to ladies looking for a husband."

Calum bit his tongue to keep from telling her that he didn't care about what other ladies liked. Violet had always enjoyed his beard.

"Your Grace, what a surprise."

Calum stiffened. Three ladies approached, peering curiously at him behind their raised fans. He recognized them instantly. They'd been friendly with Violet before her death, though she hadn't been very close with them. He hadn't seen them since the burial.

"I did not expect to see you here, Your Grace," the one in the middle said. "I thought you would have stayed out of the eye of the ton for the rest of your life."

"Come now, Mary," the lady to the left of her said lightly. "That wouldn't be fair, would it? It has been years after all."

"Yes, I suppose," Mary drawled in a tone that implied she did not agree.

Calum couldn't think of a single thing to say. His mind had emptied. All he could see was the day he had first met Violet. She had been standing with these three ladies during their first debut. Their eyes had met across the room and he had made his way over to ask her to dance...

"Let us not talk about such morbid topics," Eleanor cut in. "And if you will excuse us, ladies, but I need to speak with my nephew about something, alone."

"Of course, of course," Mary said. "We did not come to linger, only to give our greetings. Your Grace, it is good to see you."

Calum nodded stiffly. Eleanor slipped her arm through his and began pulling him away.

"How brazen that murderer to show his face."

The whisper was not said quietly enough. Calum knew that Eleanor overheard it as well. She halted for half a beat before continuing to pull him away from the three ladies and their treacherous words. But the damage was done. She'd only said what everyone else around them was thinking.

Calum was a murderer. In a fit of rage, he took things too far and tried to cover up what he did. And now his guilt kept him locked away in his manor away from the public eye.

At least they were right about one thing.

"Don't listen to them," Eleanor said softly, patting his arm in a manner that he believed she meant to be comforting. "They are bitter women who do not know what they are talking about."

"This might have been a mistake," Calum said without thinking, mostly to himself. "Stephen was right."

"Stephen was not," Eleanor insisted. "Follow me. I'll show you that—"

Calum pulled away from her suddenly. The eyes trailing them as they went along were suddenly too much to bear, like a million stones being thrown at him at once.

"I need some fresh air," he mumbled.

"Calum—"

Calum stalked away, heading in the direction of the balcony. The crowd of guests parted easily for him to go by and the murmurs followed in his wake.

He plunged out onto the shadowed balcony, drawing in a deep breath of relief when he found it empty. Hopefully, no one would be mad enough to follow him out here. He wanted to be alone. Perhaps he could attempt to pass the entirety of the ball out here?

He shouldn't have come. Stephen had warned him against it several times, telling him that it would only do more damage if he were to attempt to find a wife amidst the never-ending rumors surrounding Violet's death. But he'd listened to Eleanor instead and look what happened within minutes of his arrival.

"Calum?"

Calum gripped the balcony's railings tightly to hold back his roar of frustration. "I want to be alone, Eleanor," he pushed through gritted teeth.

"I know," she said softly. Footsteps approached him from behind. "But you have been alone for so long. I do not think that is what you need right now."

"You do not know what I need," he snapped.

But she came closer still, putting a hand on his back. His mother used to do the same thing when he was young, rubbing his back in a comforting manner whenever he felt distressed or sad. The mere touch was enough to ease some of the tension coiled tightly inside him.

"Ignore them, Calum. They know nothing. Why listen to the ramblings of the ignorant?"

Calum grunted, silently agreeing. Ignorant was the nicest way of describing them. Bad-tempered or not, he could not understand why anyone would think he would harm his late wife when it had been clear as day that he had been madly in love with her.

"Come with me," Eleanor urged. "There is someone I would like to introduce you to."

"Already?" he sighed. "Is this the reason you wanted me to attend so badly?"

"Partially," she admitted. He heard the smile in her voice.

"And since you have been so compliant with everything else, why not make this simple as well? She is already waiting for you."

Calum didn't bother to fight her. He knew it would be useless, considering the fact that she was so good at getting her way. He simply gave up on the thought of slipping away from the ball undetected and allowed her to lead him back inside, their arms linked. He tried to ignore what was being said about him as much as he could but the task grew more difficult as they delved deeper into the crowd.

"Lady Yulebridge!" came an enthusiastic gush. A small lady heavily with child came rushing forward to embrace Eleanor.

"Lady Santbury, I'm sorry to keep you waiting," Eleanor was saying. Calum hovered behind her, eyes drifting over the heads of those around them, seeing nothing and everything at the same time. Eleanor pulled him forward. "Allow me to introduce you to my nephew, His Grace Calum Hawthorn, the Duke of Thorneshire."

Calum politely bowed. "A pleasure, my lady."

Lady Santbury was a pretty lady with a healthy glow he could only assume was a result of her round stomach. She sank into a curtsy. "The pleasure is mine, Your Grace. Please, meet my niece, Miss Clarissa Wyndham."

She stepped slightly to the side and the lady who had been standing next to Lady Santbury—whom Calum had been ignoring this entire time—stepped forward. She bowed her head and sank into a curtsy that would be better given to the Prince Regent considering how deeply she lowered.

"It is a pleasure to meet you, Your Grace," she said, her voice soft and airy. She raised her head and Calum sucked in a breath.

She was a beauty. The kind of beauty that could not be denied no matter what she wore. Her dark hair was thick, in small curls piled atop her head. A few of those tendrils framed her heart-shaped face and her perfectly pink lips were curved into a slight smile. For a moment, Calum forgot what the proper thing to say or do was. But then he remembered that they were not alone, that his aunt and Lady Santbury seemed to be watching them with keen interest.

He knew what his aunt wanted to do and it wouldn't work. Miss Clarissa was certainly pretty but that wasn't enough.

"Oh, it looks as if the first set is about to begin!" Eleanor said suddenly just as the music grew a bit louder. The guests began to shift, those who intended to dance moving towards the middle of the room while the onlookers shifted to the sides.

Calum felt her eyes boring into him. He held back his resigned sigh, recognizing his duty.

"Miss Clarissa, would you like to have this dance?" he asked, his voice flat enough to show his lack of interest in the matter.

Miss Clarissa nodded, her eyes shining with something he couldn't quite decipher. "I would love to, Your Grace," she said simply and held out her hand. Calum claimed it, feeling a tingle of annoyance at what he was about to do. The last thing he wanted was to dance with another lady in the center of a room of people who had nothing good to say about him.

His aunt would hear about this later. But for now, he did what was expected of him.

Just his luck, he realized after a moment. They would be dancing the waltz.

Calum couldn't hold back his scowl any longer as he pulled her into his arms. She smelled refreshing and it distracted him from his growing irritation for a second. But then the dance began and he was forced to move to the practiced steps of the waltz, knowing that everyone was watching.

"Thank you for asking me to dance, Your Grace."

Her voice was so soft that he thought he might have imagined it for a moment. "There is no need to thank me," he said gruffly. "I did it out of duty, not because I wanted to."

"It does not matter," she said simply. "I thank you all the same. I was feeling a bit uncertain about whether I would be able to dance at all."

Without thinking, he looked down at her. As if she sensed his eyes, Miss Clarissa glanced up at the same time and their gazes met. That shadow passed in her eyes once more but before he could determine what it meant, her lips curved up into a soft smile.

"Tell me about yourself, Your Grace."

Those words shocked him so much that he nearly tripped over his feet. If she noticed the stumble, she made no indication.

Did she not know who he was? How couldn't she? Violet's death had caused such a stir that he thought all of England knew about the 'monstrous' Duke of Thorneshire.

"There is nothing to say," he said when he had recovered. "As a matter of fact, I would much rather this dance pass in silence."

"Why?" she asked, sounding genuinely curious.

That question surprised him enough that he found himself thinking about an answer without realizing it. "Do I need a reason?"

Miss Clarissa was quiet for a moment. They twirled together in those brief seconds of silence as if they had danced together a million times before. "I suppose you do not," she said at last. "Pray, let us cease this discussion and simply revel in our waltz together."

Calum nodded in agreement. But as time went on, he couldn't stop himself from looking at her again. And then he realized what it was he saw in her eyes. Sadness and fear. They lingered behind her hazel eyes like the true figure behind a mask. Perhaps he would not have recognized it if he didn't know those emotions so well himself.

What could have caused them? Why would such a beautiful lady like her gaze out in the distance as if she harbored a deep sadness that she could not contain?

For a moment, he was tempted to inquire. But he tucked that urge away, deciding that it would be better to let this set pass in silence and hope that his aunt would not attempt to introduce him to anyone else.

Before long, the dance drew to an end. As soon as they made their final steps of the waltz, Miss Clarissa stepped away from him and sank into another curtsy that was far too deep. "Thank you, Your Grace. Have a nice evening."

She didn't wait for his response. She did not even look at him as she straightened. Miss Clarissa simply turned and walked away, leaving him staring after her.

Chapter Four

Clarissa immediately made her way to the refreshments table, picking up the skirt of her dress to move quickly. Heat was crawling up her neck, her heart racing at such a rapid pace that she was a little afraid that she might collapse. She saw nothing but the table, a goal to focus on while the effects of her dance with the Duke of Thorneshire settled well into her bones.

It was only her first dance and she was such a mess!

She halted in front of the table and panicked. She needed something else to focus on. Something to distract her from this overwhelming rush of anxiousness that was creeping up on her. She'd made it this far without it and His Grace had gone and thrown her off balance.

She spotted the bowl of lemonade and all but lunged for it. In the back of her mind, she remembered that she was in public. Even though she was basically a wallflower, she had to ensure that she made no slights at all just in case someone was watching.

Clarissa took a sip of the lemonade and put a hand on against her chest in the hopes that it would calm her racing heartbeat. She couldn't understand what was happening to her. The moment the Duke of Thorneshire pulled her into his arms, she had lost all her senses. It was a wonder she'd made it through the dance without stepping on his feet at all!

Unable to help herself, Clarissa ran her gaze through the crowd. She spotted him immediately. He'd sought a corner of the room, leaning against the wall with his arms crossed and a scowl on his face. He seemed to be looking at everyone and nothing at the same time, his eyes shifting through the crowd of guests but with that faraway look as if he was not really seeing anyone.

Oh, dear goodness, he was handsome. Even from the distance, Clarissa could hardly believe it. She hadn't wanted to look directly at him out of fear that she would begin to blush.

His hair was so black it seemed to suck the light out of the room, his eyes a piercing gray that saw straight through her. He was tall. He was muscular. He was the spitting image of a devilishly handsome gentleman with a high prestige. Surely every lady in attendance would be vying for his attention in the hopes of snagging him as a husband.

Was that the reason her aunt had introduced them? Clarissa could tell that it had been planned. Martha had been looking through the guests from the moment they spoke, telling Clarissa that she should prepare herself for when the dancing commenced as if she knew that she would have a partner. There was no doubt that Martha was hoping to secure a courtship between the duke and her. The question on Clarissa's mind was, would the duke have any interest in her?

That dance gave her an answer, without a single bit of doubt. The duke couldn't care less about her. Perhaps he didn't care about anyone at all, considering the fact that he seemed to be quite miserable at the fact that he was at the ball in the first place.

"Clarissa?"

Clarissa tore her eyes away from the duke, turning to the person who approached. She blinked in surprise. "Nora?"

Nora's round brown eyes grew big with happiness. She'd always had the brightest smile, Clarissa remembered, and the years they hadn't seen each other hadn't dimmed it in the slightest.

Without warning, Nora stepped in for an embrace. Clarissa quickly set her lemonade aside before she spilled it.

"It's been so long!" Nora squealed. "I didn't think you would be here. What a surprise!"

"Yes, it is a surprise for me as well," Clarissa admitted with a laugh. The anxiousness that had sunken onto her shoulders eased now that her old friend was here. They'd once been close, but after her father died, Clarissa had lost touch with many people she'd called her friends.

Nora had been the only one who continued writing her letters. But with everything that had been going on at the time, Clarissa could hardly find the chance to respond. Three letters a week turned to one and eventually became none.

"You don't know how happy I am that you are here," Nora said amicably, as if it hadn't been over a year since they'd spoken last. That had always been Clarissa's favorite thing about Nora. She was the kind of person who held no grudges, and who always had a listening ear and a wagging tongue for those she deemed close to her. "I was quickly feeling out of place here. Lady Yulebridge is acquainted with so many important lords and ladies."

"If it is any consolation, I think you look lovely," Clarissa said honestly. Nora always believed that she was a bit plain—a notion that Clarissa would always disagree with—but she did look exceptionally pretty today.

"As do you! Is this a new dress?"

Clarissa smiled. "It is. My uncle purchased it for me. An entirely new wardrobe as well, if you can believe it."

"Oh, how lucky! Will you be entering the marriage mart then? Mother thinks that it is about time that I do the same, but I doubt this season will be any better than the others."

"Why do you say that?"

Nora shrugged. "It is my third Season, after all. If I fail, Mother will have me marry the dull, old, Earl of Hanson. If I am yet to court anyone of interest, then why would this Season be any different? There are no new faces, after all."

"Is that so?" Clarissa looked around the ballroom. She didn't know the truth of it herself. Had things been different, she would have debuted the same year as Nora. Would she have been married by now? Or lamenting the lack of options like her friend was?

"Well..." Nora hummed. "Perhaps not everyone is the same. It seems the Duke of Thorneshire has decided to show his face again."

For some reason, the mention of the duke made Clarissa's heart skip a beat. She found him again in the same spot. The scowl hadn't lifted. If anything, he seemed even more unapproachable.

"It is quite a pity," Nora sighed.

Clarissa frowned at her friend. "What is?"

"The duke, of course," she answered simply.

Clarissa' frown just deepened. "Is he already married?" she asked, masking the shadow of disappointment she felt at the notion. Perhaps that was why he'd shown no interest in her at all?

Nora looked at her as if she'd grown a third eye in the center of her forehead. "Do you mean you do not know?"

"Is there something that I should know?"

"Yes! Well, I suppose it is not surprising considering how out of touch you had become after..." Nora trailed off. It touched Clarissa's heart to see the flash of sorrow on Nora's face before she returned to her usual self.

"The duke was married," she explained, lowering her voice. "But his wife passed away five years ago."

Clarissa studied the scowl on the duke's face, remembering his obvious reluctance to dance with her. "How sad."

"Sad Perhaps for his late wife's family, but not for him."

"What do you mean?"

Nora stepped closer, leaning in for a whisper. "It is said that in a fit of rage, he killed her on their wedding night."

For a few seconds, Clarissa thought she might be jesting. There simply couldn't be any way that was true. But Nora's grim expression told her that she was utterly serious.

Still, Clarissa couldn't truly believe it. She didn't know why. She didn't know him in the slightest and their brief interaction had bordered on unsavory. Yet, as she stared at him from across the room, Clarissa wondered if he could truly harbor such violent rage deep within him.

"After her death," Nora went on, "he locked himself away in his estate. He hasn't shown his face in five years. Some say that it is because of his guilt. Others say that he only wishes to escape his judgment."

"And what do you say?" Clarissa asked her.

Nora hummed in thought before saying, "I say that there may be more to the story than we know."

Clarissa's lips tilted up in a half-smile. "It seems to me like you do not believe that the duke truly murdered his wife."

"All I'm saying is that it would be quite a shame that a man as handsome as he could do such a thing," she said with a laugh. "I am willing to give him the benefit of the doubt."

Clarissa silently agreed.

"What do you think is worse, Clarissa," Nora asked. "Being a wallflower, all but disappearing in the eyes of others? Or having everyone in attendance whisper loathsome rumours about you? I for one would take the former."

Clarissa wordlessly agreed.

***

It was too bright, too lovely of a morning. The sun shone

brightly in Eleanor's opulent garden, a gentle breeze wafting in through the bay windows of her breakfast parlor. If he was quiet enough, Calum thought he could almost hear birds singing. It was as if the universe intended to rub in his face how perfect it could be while the remains of his stable mind crumbled.

As if his dour mood wasn't difficult enough to deal with already, he felt compelled to reach for the scandal sheets even though he already knew what they could contain.

This, however, was far worse than he ever could have guessed.

His name filled the pages. His appearance at Eleanor's ball last night had stirred the ton so much that they didn't seem capable of talking about anything else. They spoke about everything from his entrance to his demeanor. They never mention in plain words what they think he did but they did state that after his five years as a recluse, he seemed to have no remorse for his actions. Miss Clarissa's name was tucked away in the last few paragraphs, saying that the lady's fall from grace must have made her desperate enough for her to dance with the rage-ridden duke.

Rage-ridden was right. At least, right now it was. Calum felt it mounting him with every line he read. He knew it was torture to do this to himself yet he could not help it. He'd only spent one night back amongst society and he was already falling into old habits, engaging in gossip.

Disgust interspersed with his anger. Calum ripped the sheets with a growl, tossing them to the floor. At that moment, Eleanor walked in.

She frowned, looking at the mess he'd made then back at him. Calum ignored her eyes, glaring out the window.

"Has something upset you, Calum?" she asked gently as she approached.

He didn't say anything, jaw clenched. But he paid attention as she bent to pick up one of the larger pieces of paper.

"I did not think you would engage in such things," she commented after a while.

"How can I not when the pages are filled with my name?" he couldn't help but snap. "I knew attending the ball was a mistake. They have nothing good to say and now, the good name I aim to protect will run rampant throughout England with malicious rumours attached."

Eleanor sighed. "I cannot say that I did not expect this to happen. The ton can be quite cruel when it concerns commenting on the lives of others. But they are only rumours, Calum. We cannot control what is said about us but we can control how we present ourselves to the world."

Calum slid his glare to her and felt a glimmer of regret when she flinched. He couldn't bring himself to soften his expression however. "Do you mean to say that I act the way that they say about me?"

"Certainly not. Only that I know of the true goodness lying underneath your gruff exterior. Eleanor paused, reaching over to hold his hand. "And perhaps Miss Clarissa does as well."

"Eleanor, don't do this," Calum said, coming to a stand. He'd been dreading this conversation since he saw through his aunt's attempts last night. He should have left early this morning to avoid it altogether.

"She thinks you are rather nice," Eleanor attempted to say. At his sharp, incredulous look, she added, "At least, that is what her aunt tells me."

"A polite thing to say about a stranger, I'm sure," Calum muttered. "I doubt she will think the same when she sees her name being sullied all because of one dance with me."

"Miss Clarissa is no stranger to the wagging tongues of the ton," Eleanor explained. "Her family was once prosperous, you see. An admirable feat considering the fact that her father was only a baron. But it seemed he had mismanaged their wealth in the latter years of his life and, after he died, Miss Clarissa and her family were plunged into destitution. And let me say that the ton was no more gentle on her than they would be with anyone else." Eleanor raised her brows hopefully. "Don't you think it might be a good idea to secure a match between you two? It would be rather beneficial."

Calum swallowed, his irritation tingling his skin. He crossed over to the hearth, hoping that the distance would at least dampen the scowl that had crept over his face. "How exactly will it benefit me to marry a ruined lady with no dowry?" *As beautiful as she is*, he added inwardly.

"You and I both know that you do not care about one's

dowry, Calum," Eleanor said, sounding a bit weary. "You are one of the wealthiest dukes in England. The only thing you need now is a companion, and someone to bear you a son."

"I do not need either. Nor do I need to endure this conversation any longer. I have humoured you enough Eleanor."

Calum stalked towards the door. He hoped that she would leave him well alone but it was wishful thinking considering the fact that she was almost as stubborn as he was.

"Why don't you attend dinner at Lord and Lady Santbury's manor?" she asked hurriedly, coming to a stand. Calum paused in his tracks, his annoyance and frustration mounting. "It will be a relaxed environment where we can further assess the compatibility between Miss Clarissa and you."

"What lady would want to marry a presumed murderer?" he snarled, bitterness churning in his gut.

"Calum, you're not—"

"Enough!" Before he could stop himself, he grabbed the nearest thing to him, which happened to be a Chinese vase, and threw it across the room. The moment it collided on the floor, splintering into a dozen pieces, Calum realized he might have taken it too far. But it was Eleanor's horrified gasp that filled him with sharp regret.

He didn't look at her, stalking out the room instead. The moment he was out of the parlor, he leaned against the door, resting the back of his head on the cool wood.

No wonder others thought he was a tempestuous man. Had he always been like this?

Calum closed his eyes, his mind wandering back to the days when he had been slower to anger and quicker to laugh. Violet would have hated the man he was now. How ironic it was that her death had been what created it.

A sob broke through his reverie. Calum straightened, realizing that he was hearing it from the other side of the door. Eleanor was crying.

Horror descended on him. Calum turned to the door and hesitated. A part of him wanted to pretend he didn't hear it and leave. It would be easier that way. Running from everyone for years had become simple.

But his self-loathing at what he'd caused forced him back

inside the parlor. Eleanor sat where he'd left her and she did not hesitate to turn her tear-filled eyes to him. Calum felt his throat grow thick as he made his way to her side. He reclaimed his chair, not knowing what to do.

At last, he said, "Forgive me. I don't know what came over me."

"You are forgiven," Eleanor said without a moment of hesitation. She wiped her tears.

Calum avoided her eyes. "I shall attend the dinner." She said nothing. He added, "And I shall make an effort with Miss Clarissa if that will appease you."

"It most certainly will." He could hear the relief in her voice. She stood and made her way to him, pressing a tender kiss on his cheek. "Thank you, Calum. You will not regret it."

Calum sincerely doubted it. But he was content to pretend that he would for now, if that was what it took to keep the smile on Eleanor's face.

Chapter Five

It had been two days since the ball. Two days of relative peace before this was brought to Clarissa's attention.

It was all because of Nora. Her lovely, talkative, eager friend had written to her just this morning. The moment Clarissa unveiled the lengthy pages that Nora had written, she'd broken into a smile, content to fall back into the usual practice of writing to her dear friend. That smile had slowly slipped from her face when, a few paragraphs in, Nora asked her if she'd seen what was being said in the scandal sheets about her.

Clarissa never cared to read such things before. Falling into destitution had made engaging ton gossip even less appealing. Now, she wished she hadn't been curious enough to seek this issue of scandal sheets herself.

Beastly Duke Debuts New Bride

She gripped her teacup so tightly that her knuckles went white. Her breath hitched in her throat. Her stomach churned with the uncertainty she had been trying to ignore ever since she attended the ball. Her entry into society had been sullied by the duke's name.

The scandal sheets spoke mostly about him. She was only mentioned a few times but they were far from favorable. Clarissa read the line about her alleged desperation since her 'fall from grace' five times.

To make matters worse, she wasn't alone. She should have taken this to her chambers to read it in secret. Instead, she'd foolishly brought it into the drawing room where her aunt, her mother, and her sister were there to see it as well.

"This is horrible!" Louisa cried. She picked up one of the sheets, gripping it so tightly that it crumpled in her hand. "How could they say these things about you?"

"It is not that bad," Clarissa murmured even though she did not believe her own words. They'd had nothing good to say about the duke and she was being dragged into it. Clarissa knew firsthand how the reputation of one person was enough to overshadow another's. She and her family had endured the same thing after her father's death, even though they had nothing to do with what had happened to them.

"It is terrible!" Louisa looked distraught. It was a far cry from how excited she had been to read what was being said just mere minutes ago. "They think that you are meant to marry a man who had killed his previous wife! Nothing good can come of this!"

Olivia stirred. As usual, Clarissa focused her attention on her. She looked at her mother, watching as a slow frown came over her face. Olivia turned her head slowly to look at Louisa. "What did you say?"

Louisa thinned her lips. She hesitated and Clarissa hoped she wouldn't say anything about it. Martha seemed content to sip her tea as if there wasn't a care in the world. Had she known that this would happen?

"It is nothing, Mother—" Louisa began.

"A murderer?" Olivia whispered, her voice tinged with horror. It was truly alarming to watch a woman who had worn nothing but a blank expression for so long look so terrified and outraged in a matter of seconds. Clarissa gripped her teacup tighter, her tea long cold.

Olivia got to her feet. The megrims that had been plaguing her since her fainting spell seemed not to bother her now. She whirled to Martha, who bit gingerly into a piece of cake as if they were having a nice discussion about the weather.

"How could you do this to my daughter?" Olivia screamed. Her face went red as she took threatening steps towards Martha. "How could you let my innocent daughter near that murderous beast?"

Martha regarded her evenly. "I did not let her near a murderous beast. I let her near the Duke of Thorneshire. And I know his family long enough to be assured of his innocence in that matter."

Olivia scoffed. "Innocence? Everyone knows what he has done! Goodness, had I known that this was your intention all along, I would have attended the ball with Clarissa myself. Is this what you wanted? For her reputation to be so thoroughly damaged that she would stand no hope of being married?"

"That is the last thing I want," Martha snapped firmly. "I wish for nothing else but for Clarissa to find a good match. And that is exactly what I believe the Duke of Thorneshire is. A good match."

"You may be the only one in England to think such a thing." Olivia collapsed in her chair, raising her hand to her face. Louisa rushed to her side. "Oh, she is ruined. Absolutely ruined."

Clarissa's throat went dry as she watched her mother swoon again. She didn't know what to do. All she could think about was the duke's eyes when they'd caught hers during their dance. A troubled look. One of pain. One she knew far too well and had recognized instantly.

"I understand your concern, Olivia," Martha went on. "But through my friendship with His Grace's aunt, Lady Yulebridge, I've come to learn that the Duke of Thorneshire had been quite in love with his wife and had nothing to do with her death. Those are just foolish and malicious rumours."

"But..." Louisa spoke up uncertainly, worry set deep in her brow. "Surely the rumours stemmed from somewhere. Would they have made up such things on a whim?"

Martha gave her a pitying look. Clarissa felt the same way. Louisa, her dear sheltered and optimistic sister, couldn't truly understand the viciousness of the ton. It only took one person to speak with the right conviction for others to believe. They did not care to know the truth. So long as it made for good conversation over tea.

"Believe me when I say, Louisa, that it is utterly untrue," Martha told her. "And perhaps you will find that out for yourself, because I have invited him and his aunt over for dinner this evening."

Louisa looked unconvinced. Olivia straightened, having recovered enough to say, "I will not allow you to bring that beast near my daughters."

Martha sighed heavily, as if she realized that she was fighting a losing battle. Clarissa stared down at the scandal sheets before her. Instead of the words, she saw the duke standing in the corner of the room with his arms crossed. At the time, she'd thought he looked rather fearsome despite his handsomeness, like a man prepared to throw his fists up if someone dared to speak wrongly to him.

But now she wondered if those fists would be in defense. If he was just a man who faced the world's accusations about him as he harbored the truth deep within.

"The duke seems like a broken gentleman mourning his bride," she said without thought. "Not a soulless beast."

It took her a few moments to realize that they were all staring at her with shock. Clarissa met her mother's eyes. "It may not be as bad as you think, Mother. And besides, I did not have a pristine reputation from the start."

Olivia's eyes went wide. Slowly she pulled away from Louisa and Clarissa watched her fall back into an unresponsive state, like drapes falling around windows. Without another word, she turned back to the window.

Louisa sighed silently and went back to Clarissa's side. "This is not how I thought the beginning of your Season would go," she murmured thoughtfully.

Clarissa silently agreed. But she would be lying if she said she'd expected it to be far better. Clarissa knew how it felt to wear the badge of disgrace around for others to see, to be judged before others got to know her. Louisa had remained untouched by the vicious tongue of others but Clarissa knew from the moment that she decided to attend that it would not be easy. She hadn't thought it would be because of an allegedly ill-tempered duke, however, and not her own broken reputation.

"Clarissa," Martha said as she stood, wearing a small smile. "Would you like to join me for our afternoon walk?"

She nodded, even though the only thing she wished to do now was retire to her room. She stood and followed Martha out of the room. She was forced to walk slowly due to Martha's waddle, but she liked the silence. It gave her time to think, to mentally prepare for what was to come later that evening.

They'd made it all the way out to the gardens before Martha decided to break the quiet. "Are you afraid of the duke, Clarissa?"

Her answer came easily. "No, I am not. He has given me no reason to fear him."

"Good." Martha sounded pleased. She caressed her stomach as she walked, a thoughtful look on her face. "I think it is rather unfair that everyone judges him so soundly. Half of these people do not know him. They only repeat what has been told to them."

"If you believe in that logic, Aunt, then you should not blame my mother for not believing what you have told her."

As soon as the words were out of her mouth, Clarissa

regretted them. She'd always made sure to mind her tongue around her uncle and aunt, not daring to overstep in any manner that might get them put out. Sometimes she wished that she could be as carefree as Louisa was.

But then Martha laughed and the tight knot of tension in the base of her neck diffused. "You're right, Clarissa. That is rather unfair of me. I should give them a chance to meet the duke themselves. Then they will know."

"Is that why you wished to speak with me?" Clarissa asked, a little hesitant.

"Yes, but I also wanted some fresh air," Martha confessed. "I think the duke and you will make a lovely match. As does his aunt, which is why we arranged for you to meet at the ball. To be honest, I did expect the backlash that you received, but I think the risk would be worth the award."

"You speak about marriage, Aunt, but there is nothing that I can offer the duke to make him consider one with me. He did not seem interested in me at all during our dance."

"It has been some time since he has been in the public eye. I'm sure with time, he will relax. You are a beautiful girl with a lovely personality. What is there not to like?"

Clarissa nearly laughed at that. She couldn't count on all ten fingers the things that made her unsuitable for marriage. She was too serious, for one, and bearing the responsibility of her family's future made that no better. Not to mention the fact that she tended to speak candidly without thought, which was not often received very well.

Clarissa held her tongue as her aunt continued. "Worry not about the benefits he will receive through the marriage. He is wealthy, he is well-connected, and he is handsome. Those are the only three things one looks for in a husband."

"His demeanour makes me hesitate," Clarissa confessed. "What if he truly does harbour a bad temper?"

"You are a discerning woman," Martha assured her. "I know that he does not and you will see yourself in time." She stopped, resting a hand on Clarissa's arm. "I will not try to push you into a marriage. It is your decision in the end. All I ask is that you give the duke a chance during the dinner this evening."

Clarissa nodded. She'd already intended on doing just that

without her aunt's suggestion. There was something about the duke that made her want to peer closer, even though that may be akin to taunting a lion. Clarissa didn't want her face to be bitten off but she also wanted to see behind the layers for the true man underneath.

She only hoped that seeing him wouldn't turn her into a bumbling mess like last time.

***

The Miller townhouse was an impressive sight, a sure indication that the Earl and Countess of Santbury had done quite well for themselves. Upon Calum and Eleanor's arrival, they were even greeted by a host of footmen and maids who bowed and escorted them to the front door.

The butler was no less reverent and the sight of him only set Calum's teeth further on edge. It had been bad enough that he'd dreaded this since agreeing to it, but now that he was here, they were treating him as if he were the Prince Regent himself. Nothing good could come of this. Eleanor however beamed as if she could not be happier.

"Smile, Calum," she whispered, nudging him in the side. "You look rather unpleasant when you scowl like that."

"That is my aim," Calum muttered back and she tutted disapprovingly. Calum sighed and resigned himself to a slightly more pleasant expression.

The butler brought them to the parlor where Lord and Lady Santbury apparently awaited, alongside their wards, including Miss Clarissa. For some reason, the thought of seeing her again made Calum uneasy. It wasn't her beauty that threw him, he thought to himself. At least, he hoped it wasn't. He'd met plenty of lovely ladies during his life—though perhaps not many as heart-wrenchingly gorgeous as Miss Clarissa—so he didn't think that could be the reason why seeing her made his palms itch.

He tucked the feeling aside as the butler stepped into the parlor and announced their arrival. Eleanor entered first, smiling broadly. Calum followed closely behind.

The first person he saw was Miss Clarissa. There were more persons than he'd expected and he felt a familiar twinge of wariness now that he knew he was meant to dine with them all. But the feeling crept up slowly on him, buffeted by his failure to breathe the moment he locked eyes with Miss Clarissa.

She rose to a stand, hands clasped before her. She bore a small, pleasant smile but her bright hazel eyes shone with something unintelligible. It felt as if she was seeing something that he did not want her to see, something he had spent too long hiding from others. Calum tore his gaze away but could not stop from running it down the rest of her, drinking in the way that pale blue evening dress clung to her slim frame.

"Your Grace, Lady Yulebridge, it is a pleasure." A tall, broad-shouldered man approached them with a wide grin. Calum snapped his eyes to him. "My wife has spoken about you two so often that it feels like I've already known you for some time now."

"As she does with you, my lord," Eleanor said with a laugh. "Thank you for your kind invitation to dine with you and your lovely family, Lord Santbury."

"No, no, you honour us by attending." Then Calum felt the earl's attention shift to him for a brief moment before he said. "Please allow me to introduce you to my family."

The rest of them drew nearer, stepping forward one by one. "This is my sister, Lady Olivia Wyndham, the Dowager Baroness of Quelshire," he introduced. "And these are her daughters, Miss Clarissa and Miss Louisa."

The younger of the two curtsied shyly. "It is nice to meet you," she said in a low tone. She could not be older than ten-and-six years and, despite her quiet voice, she stared at Calum with open curiosity.

Calum tried not to glare at her, annoyed that he was already being subject to such scrutiny. "A pleasure," he pushed out.

Miss Clarissa must have noticed his discomfort because she nudged her sister in her side. Louisa looked at her with wide eyes murmuring, "What? Did I do something wrong?"

For a moment, the pleasant lady he'd met at the ball disappeared the moment she gave her sister a stern look. Calum didn't know what she whispered back to her. But Miss Louisa lowered her gaze and Miss Clarissa faced him with that perfectly, polite smile. "It is a pleasure to see you again, Your Grace."

Calum didn't respond, only stared at her. The silence quickly grew uncomfortable until Lady Santbury cut in. "Then shall we make our way to the dining room?"

Eleanor and Lord Santbury were happy to agree. Only after did Calum realize that the baroness had not said a word to him. Her face was a blank slate and she moved slowly, like she was not certain where she was going. As she passed him though, her eyes snapped to him and hatred filled them.

He'd come to expect something like that this evening so he tried not to let it bother him too much.

They all filed out of the parlor and the butler, who apparently had been waiting outside the room, began leading the way to the dining room. Calum trailed behind them, his gaze falling on Miss Clarissa once more. She walked with her back straight and her chin raised, the picture of the perfect lady. With her hair curled atop her head, looking so heavy that he wondered if her neck pained her, he realized that she wore no jewelery. Was that because of her family's destitution?

Without warning, Clarissa turned to look at him. Calum struggled not to look away. Her eyes were piercing enough that it felt like she saw right through him, yet gentle enough to make him think that she did not mind what she saw.

It was unnerving, to say the least.

She looked back in front and said nothing to him as they entered the dining room. Calum watched with veiled annoyance as everyone ensured that he was seated next to Miss Clarissa. Eleanor flashed him a look that clearly told him to 'play nice'.

He didn't know how to play nice. Not anymore. He'd snapped at his valet *again* while getting ready for the dinner earlier and it was a wonder the man hadn't resigned yet.

The first course of white soup was served. Lord and Lady Santbury fell into easy and open conversation that could be enjoyed by anyone. Miss Louisa took advantage of that fact, her earlier suspicion of him disappearing. She smiled and talked as if she'd forgotten he was there at all. Lady Olivia sat stiffly, eyes on the table, hand moving mechanically as she stirred her soup.

Miss Clarissa did not say a word.

Calum did not mind. He did not intend to speak either. He'd promised his aunt that he would attend the dinner, to consider a match with Miss Clarissa. He didn't have to take it any further than that.

"Do you like poetry, Your Grace?"

Again, Miss Clarissa's voice was so soft that he almost didn't realize that she'd spoken. When he glanced at her, he noticed that she was staring up at him.

His lips moved on their own accord. "Perhaps."

"Perhaps?" she mused aloud. "That is quite an ambiguous response."

"I am an ambiguous man."

"I do not doubt it." There was a lull. Calum thought she might have gotten the hint that he did not wish to talk, since his standoffish demeanor had not been enough. But then she said, "I like them. Poems. More than others might, considering they are the only good parts of my day."

Calum grunted.

She went on. "I wish to have a conversation with you. The only way I know how is to find common interest. And the only thing I am interested in, is poetry."

Calum slid his gaze to her again, fighting his frown of confusion. Could she not see that he was in no mood to speak with her? She ate her soup casually, looking up to meet his eyes with open curiosity. She knew that he did not care to answer her, he realized, and yet she continued.

"On my better days, I rather admire Lord Byron's verses." He pushed the words out with reluctance.

But the change he saw in her was almost instant. She straightened, eyes brightening with intrigue, her first real smile touching her lips though it was small. "Truly? Lord Byron is my favourite poet. Which of his poems do you like the most?"

This wasn't how he'd expected the night to go. He thought he would be suffering through every second with a barely disguised scowl on his face until it was time to leave. Yet here he was, considering the poems he hadn't read in years to give a proper answer.

"*Epitaph to a Dog*," he answered at last.

Miss Clarissa nodded as if that made perfect sense. "I enjoy that one as well. As a matter of fact, I read it quite a few times before dinner. I am writing my own poems, you see, and thought it would be good emotional inspiration."

"I see." It was an easy response, a natural end to a small conversation. But Calum spoke without thinking. "Is it your favourite poem of his as well?"

"No, it is not," she answered immediately. "My favourite happens to be *Maid of Athens, ere we part*."

"I see."

"Do you like it?"

Calum tensed. He hadn't read poems since Violet. "I do not know it well."

"Then would you like to borrow my copy?" she asked without hesitation. "I would love to get your thoughts on it."

Calum considered it for a moment. "I suppose that would be fine."

"Marvelous." And then that smile returned, genuine and a little bigger than usual. He wondered what it would be like to witness one as full and as bright as her sister's.

The others did not seem to mind that they did not partake in any conversation. If anything, they were content to ignore them, no doubt wanting to encourage what was happening between them. Calum couldn't deny that it was easier to speak with Miss Clarissa than he thought. She asked questions with no expectations in her voice, like she would not mind if he did not respond to her. Like she would understand if he didn't.

Would it really be so bad to marry her?

The thought brought on a vicious wave of disgust directed at himself. He felt like a traitor to Violet's memory for even thinking such a thing. How could he stay true to her if he gave himself to another?

But he would not be giving himself. Calum glanced at Miss Clarissa from the corner of his eye. Miss Clarissa seemed nice enough so sharing her company may not be so bad. All he had to do was have her bear him an heir. He didn't have to give his heart, wouldn't even be able to if he tried. That way, he would fulfill his one true duty as a duke while remaining faithful to Violet.

It was nothing more than a business transaction, the marriage certificate, the contract. It would not be so bad, would it?

His mental conundrum continued all the way through to the dessert course. Only then, when it felt as if he'd come to a decision, did he feel inclined to eat.

Chapter Six

It had been two days since their dinner with the Duke of Thornshire and Lady Yulebridge and Clarissa had not been able to get him out of her head. It bothered her. She had other things to focus on, after all. The duke had made it clear as day that he had no interest in her and that there were no hopes of a marriage between them. Clarissa had put that idea out of her head that night, despite her aunt's optimism on the matter.

And yet there she sat, trying to focus on her writing and failing. She sighed, gazing out the window. She'd sought the company of the others since they were gathered in the drawing room like usual, rather than seeking solace in the library. Clarissa had hoped that it would distract her from all thoughts of the duke.

But everyone was consumed in their own tasks. Olivia sat in her usual spot, staring unseeingly out the window. Martha had her embroidery hoop, making quick work of a small lovely flower. And Louisa, to Clarissa's surprise, was engrossed in a book. It was an unusual sight considering the fact that Louisa was not one to stay still.

Everyone was quiet, which Clarissa would have liked under normal circumstances. But thinking about the duke made things far from normal. She couldn't understand why he remained on her mind when he'd made it so clear that he did not care about her in the slightest. Their conversation had only been to humor her persistent attempts at making a connection, not because he truly cared to engage.

The door opened and the butler entered, bowing briefly to Martha before making his way to Olivia's side. That piqued Clarissa's interest. She watched as he handed over what looked like the newspaper. Olivia came back to the present, accepting the newspaper and not unfolding it until the butler was out of the room.

Clarissa frowned. Her mother had never cared to read the *Times* her entire time here. Why would she be interested now?

Clarissa glanced at her aunt and her sister. Louisa did not seem to notice what was happening. Martha's eyes were on Olivia, though her fingers skillfully continued threading her embroidery hoop.

Olivia read quietly for a while. And then she bolted upright. It still alarmed Clarissa to see it. Her mother had been so dull and lifeless for so long that watching her move and act almost normally felt odd.

"Look at this!" Olivia hissed. She marched over to Martha, throwing the newspaper down. Only then did Clarissa realize that it was a copy of the scandal sheets. "Look what your meddling has done!"

Calmly, Martha bent to pick it up. Louisa put her book aside, frowning worriedly between the two of them. "What is it?" she asked. "Is it about Clarissa again?"

After a moment, Martha nodded and simply said, "It would appear so."

"Someone noticed the duke calling on us that evening and now everyone believes that there is some truth to what was said before. That Clarissa truly is the desperate new bride of the beastly duke."

Louisa gasped. She unceremoniously took the scandal sheets from Martha's hands, reading them for herself with wide eyes. Martha only continued her embroidery.

"Do not listen to the gossip, Olivia," she said calmly. "It will only cause you distress."

"How can it not when it involves my eldest daughter? And your attitude towards this terrible situation is very telling."

"That is because I know better than to care about the ramblings of those who know nothing about what is truly going on. You will overwhelm yourself if you continue like this, Olivia. Please, allow it to be."

Olivia's face only went red. A tight knot of unease unfurled in Clarissa's stomach at the tension quickly rising in the air. She straightened, about to stand and attempt to calm her mother down. But at that moment, she heard the telltale sound of wheels crunching over gravel.

All their heads turned at the same time. Louisa shot out of the settee and rushed to the window Clarissa was sitting beside. They both peered through it, catching a glimpse of the driveway and the carriage that pulled within. It stopped before it went out of sight and, to her utter surprise, the Duke of Thorneshire's imposing figure emerged.

He looked far too handsome to wear such an unpleasant expression, Clarissa thought. Louisa was talking but she hardly focused on what was being said. She could only watch as the duke helped Lady Yulebridge out of the carriage. Unlike her nephew, the dowager viscountess wore a happy smile.

Clarissa's heart fluttered in her chest as she watched the duke and the dowager viscountess walk away from the carriage and out of sight. She thought that the dinner would be the last time she saw him, considering his demeanor towards her. Was his aunt dragging him to visit her yet again?

Clarissa didn't like the thought of that. If she were to take a husband, or engage in courtship, she would rather he not have a perpetually sour disposition in her presence. She didn't want to share in his company if he made it so clear that he did not want to share in hers.

Even so, she braced herself for what was to come. "The duke is here," Louisa was saying, her voice filled with trepidation and enthusiasm. Olivia skulked back to her chair just as the door opened.

"My ladies, Lady Yulebridge has come to pay a visit," the butler announced. He stepped away to allow the dowager viscountess in. Clarissa held her breath, waiting for broad shoulders to brush past the threshold.

The duke never came. Instead, Lady Yulebridge came tittering up to them with a broad smile. "I hope I am not intruding on your peaceful afternoon," she said to the room.

Martha was the first to engage. "My peaceful afternoon has suddenly grown much better now that you are here. To what do we owe the pleasure?"

"Good afternoon, Lady Yulebridge," Louisa spoke up politely. "Did the Duke of Thorneshire not come with you?"

"He did," she responded. "But he has decided to speak with Lord Santbury first."

Louisa frowned. Olivia still did not acknowledge her. "About what?"

"Louisa," Clarissa spoke up quickly. "That is private and none of your concern."

Lady Yulebridge turned her attention to Clarissa with eyes

filled with pride. "Ah, such a lovely lady you are, Miss Clarissa. But to answer your question, Miss Louisa, I do not know. But it is a bit of good news, I hope. But enough of that. Have you heard of Lady Laines' upcoming ball?"

Just like that, they fell into an easy conversation. After a while, Louisa joined in, her naturally talkative trait drawn to someone as welcoming as Lady Yulebridge. Clarissa did not say anything, her mind still lingering on what she'd said about the duke. Curiosity nagged at her. It plagued her so soundly that she was almost tempted to go to her uncle's study to eavesdrop.

After what felt like ages, there was another knock on the door and the butler entered. His eyes fell on her. "Pardon the intrusion, my lady, but Lord Santbury requests your presence in his study."

Clarissa shielded her expression even as her heart hammered against her chest. She nodded and, without a word, made her way to the door, the eyes of the others following her the entire way. As she made her way to the study, she let her anxiousness seep out. She bit her bottom lip, putting a hand to her racing heart to try and calm it. Every time she tried to think about what they could have called her about, her mind went still, her apprehension paralyzing her.

Was this it? Would her uncle finally give up on her after making such a mess of her Season already?

Clarissa carefully erected her walls and put her mask back in place as she reached the door of the study. She knocked and waited for her uncle's deep voice to beckon her to enter from the other side.

Clarissa slipped into the room and tried not to look at the duke standing to the right of the room. It was a difficult feat, one she failed within seconds. Quickly, and hopefully casually, she glanced at him. One look at his shadowed scowl made her fear triple.

"Uncle? You wished to see me?"

"Yes, Clarissa. Have a seat."

She hesitated at the door. She did not want to sit or to relax. Whatever bad news that was about to come, she wanted to take standing.

But she heeded her uncle's request and claimed the chair

across from his desk. She glanced at the duke again without thinking and her breath hitched in her throat when she saw how intensely he was staring at her.

"The Duke of Thorneshire has brought an interesting proposal, Clarissa," her uncle began, his tone light enough to lift some of the unease weighing on her chest. "He has come to ask for your hand in marriage."

Clarissa didn't dare move a muscle. She felt her shock and disbelief melting through her perfectly crafted mask. "For what in return?" she asked after a long moment of thought.

Robert chuckled. He turned to face the duke. "What did I say? I told you that she was an astute woman and that she would see right through us."

Clarissa didn't dare to look at the duke this time. She kept her eyes on her uncle as she said, "I know you well, Uncle. You like to create suspense with your announcements but there is always more to the matter."

"You are right about that," he confessed. "He has proposed that a marriage be arranged between you two and in return, he shall pay your father's debt as well as secure the futures of your mother and sister. I did tell him that I am more than happy to care for my sister and my niece for as long as I need to, but he has insisted."

Clarissa still kept herself painfully still. "So I am to marry the duke?"

"No, no, I called you here to inform you of his request, Clarissa. It is not an order. You are free to accept him or deny him as you wish."

She absorbed those words with a slow nod. It was hard to come to terms with what was being said. The duke wanted to marry her. All this time she thought he did not care about her and yet he had come all the way here to ask her uncle for permission to marry her.

Carefully, she shifted in her chair to face him, meeting his stormy gray eyes. As usual, they were filled with such troubled pain, hiding behind a thin layer of displeasure. Did he not realize how obvious he was? How could anyone look this man in the eye and think that he had done anything they were accusing him of?

He was dangling her only wish in front of her eyes. Clarissa wondered if he knew how much he was saving her. He must have if he offered to clear her family's debt. It must be a small price to pay for him and for what? To marry someone like her? Was it because he thought he had no other option?

"You seem to be thinking quite hard about this," he spoke, breaking her from her thoughts.

Clarissa nodded. "I am. It is a big decision to make."

"I do not see why it should take you this long," he grunted, barely concealing his irritation. "You wish to be married, do you not? And I am offering you that and more."

Clarissa regarded him as calmly as she could manage. "What do you gain from this arrangement, Your Grace?"

"I only need to continue my family's lineage, nothing more. You seem more than capable of fulfilling that task."

Which meant that she was the only woman who cared to speak to him at all. Clarissa nodded in understanding. It was foolish to hesitate, she realized. Yes, the duke may not like her but at least he was not a cruel man, as far as she knew. And he was not only offering marriage but financial security and comfort. He was erasing all the things that had caused anxiety and fear in her for so long. She would be a fool to turn him down, especially considering the fact that her own shoddy reputation would make it difficult for her to receive such a proposal from any other man.

"I accept," she said at last.

The duke raised his chin slightly. She could have sworn she saw his shoulders relax as if in relief. Had he been fearful that she would reject him?

The mere idea had her peering closely at him. He didn't look away from her and, for a moment, she forgot that they were not alone.

Her uncle clapped his hands loudly, making her jolt. "Marvelous!" he exclaimed. "What a joyous occasion. This has worked out far more quickly than I thought it would, wouldn't you say, Clarissa?"

Clarissa managed a nod, a little unsettled by the duke's ever-present stare. "Yes, I suppose it has."

"You should go and inform the others of what is to come. His Grace and I have more things to discuss."

"Yes, Uncle." Clarissa stood, carefully turning towards the

door without looking at the duke again.

But he spoke, making her stop in her tracks. "I will acquire a special license so that we may be wed by the end of the week."

Clarissa's heart fluttered at the thought. "A sound idea, Your Grace," she responded without turning and then she left the room, letting out the breath she had been unknowingly holding.

She slowly made her way back to the drawing room, her mind a jumbled mess. It was hard to believe that after vying for something for so long, this was her reaction to it. No happiness, no relief. All she could think about was a pair of stormy gray eyes that hid shadows of pain.

The moment she entered the drawing room, the conversation halted and they all looked at her, including Olivia.

Clarissa revealed what had happened in quick words. And then Olivia fainted.

Chapter Seven

The rest of the week passed quickly and in a blur. Calum spent his time doing only two things—acquiring the special license and hiding it from Stephen.

It was a difficult feat considering his cousin was involved in nearly everything that involved him. Calum had to pretend he was more disinterested in conversation than normal and hoped that Stephen would not question him about the time he was spending with Eleanor. Stephen vehemently disapproved of the notion of Calum remarrying. It would be easier if he didn't know that Calum was already planning to do just that.

Before he knew it, he was in his chambers getting ready for the wedding that was about to happen. Calum snorted to himself at the thought. 'Wedding' was too nice a word for what was about to happen. His wedding day with Violet had been beautiful, surrounded by their loved ones and many other acquaintances of the ton. They'd exchanged vows in the garden of his estate, love shining in their eyes as they held hands. What he was about to endure was nothing compared to that. Nothing but another business transaction.

Still, the thought of seeing Miss Clarissa again gave him pause. He hadn't seen her since that day in her uncle's office when she'd looked at him as if she could see right through him. He'd realized at that moment that he could not tell what she was thinking. She was the first person he'd ever met who could shield her inner thoughts so easily, without cracking for a moment. It bothered him as much as it intrigued him.

For some reason, the thought of her sped up his movements. He'd sent word for his valet not to assist him this morning, wanting to spend some time alone with his thoughts. As a result, it took a much longer time to get dressed. But at last, he finished buttoning his embroidered waistcoat and turned to look at himself in the mirror.

Calum could not remember the last time he'd seen himself look this put together.

No, he could remember the last time. He just did not want to.

With a growl of disgust, he whirled away from the mirror and stalked out of the room. The moment he stepped out into the hallway, he ran into his valet.

Fear instantly filled the other man's eyes. He even began to shake, taking two steps back.

"What are you doing here?" Calum asked gruffly. "I thought I told you that I was not in need of your services."

"I-I know, Your Grace," he stammered. "But it was taking such a while for you to get dressed that I thought that you—" He broke off as if he just realized what he was saying and bowed deeper.

Calum frowned. He'd come here to help him? Even after how horribly Calum had treated him these past few weeks?

He regarded the valet's trembling frame and felt a shadow of remorse. He couldn't revel in his fear this time. It was easy before, when he was content to play the part of the monster that everyone thought him to be. But it felt different when he was receiving such consideration when he'd been nothing but cruel.

An apology rushed to the tip of his tongue. Calum only stared at the man, not knowing how to voice it. There was too much to apologize for. Surely there weren't enough words for him to get them all out!

In the end, all he said was, "You are dismissed."

As usual, the valet scrambled away. Calum wondered how he'd intended to provide any assistance when he could not even look him in the eye. He watched as he left then heaved a sigh. This day was already quite burdensome.

He continued along his way to the drawing room where the ceremony—if they could even call it that—would begin. On the way there, Calum ran into Mrs. Dawson. She regarded him with a cool look.

"Mr. Stephens looks as if he has just seen a ghost," she commented.

Calum frowned. "Mr. Stephens?"

"Mr. Frank Stephens," she said. "Your valet."

Calum cringed inwardly. He hadn't cared to know the name of his valet since he'd been employed shortly after Violet's death. The outside world hadn't mattered to Calum then.

"Why are you telling me this?" Calum asked her, continuing

down the hallway.

"Because he'd informed me of his intentions to go and check in on you," she said. She fell in step with him. "Only to look so shaken coming back that I wonder if you'd said or done something."

"Haven't I always?" Calum drawled. He was only tolerating this conversation because it was Mrs. Dawson. She was like a mother to him, one who perfectly skirted the line between servant and friend.

Her lips thinned in quiet disapproval. But she would not reprimand him. Not that she needed words to do that. Calum felt shame rush through him.

She stepped closer, brushing at something on his waistcoat. "That aside, Your Grace, you look quite dashing. I am pleased to see you taking such a positive step for your future."

"It is for your future as well. Once she becomes the mistress of the manor, you will not feel the need to come to me as often about any matters concerning the manor."

"I do not come to you," she stated matter-of-factly. "I got to Mr. Huntington."

Calum huffed what nearly sounded like a laugh. "Fair enough. And where is Stephen? He has not returned, has he?"

"As far as I know, he is still in London visiting your properties there. I do not think he will return until the marriage has been finalised."

"Will you not ask about why I am keeping this a secret from him?"

"I do not need to, Your Grace."

Calum let out a breath through his nose. "Is that so? I find it hard to believe that he would tell you why he is so opposed to the idea."

"He has not, Your Grace. Mr. Huntington does not speak with the help. It simply does not matter to me because I am happy you are doing it anyway. This will be good for you."

There it was. The words he certainly did not want to hear. Nothing about this was good save for the simple goal of bearing an heir.

He didn't bother to voice those thoughts aloud. Calum was drawn to stubborn people, he realized, and Mrs. Dawson was no different. Her feelings on the matter would not change.

She touched him lightly on the arm. "The others are waiting for you in the drawing room. You have a beautiful bride, Your Grace."

I know.

His response whispered through his mind and nearly blurted from his lips. Calum nodded stiffly and turned away before he said something he shouldn't. Now he felt a little frazzled, like he might be making a mistake.

It was too late to stop anything. By the time he made it to the drawing room, Eleanor—who had been waiting outside the door—rushed to his side. She began fussing over him, telling him how handsome he was and that everyone was waiting anxiously inside. She took him by the hand, pressed a kiss to his cheek, and told him how proud she was that he was making this decision.

Calum tried to use some of her enthusiasm to mask the unease coiling tightly within him. It felt as if Violet's spirit was lingering nearby, watching him with eyes of betrayal.

He tucked the feeling away and entered the drawing room. Just as his aunt had said, Miss Clarissa's family was already waiting within. The vicar was there as well, talking with Lady Santbury. Lady Quelshire fanned herself, eyes rolling to the back of her head as if she was about to fall unconscious at any moment. Miss Louisa was by her side, holding her mother's hand, watching her carefully with a slightly worried expression.

They all looked at him as he entered. Calum ignored them but their weighty gazes did not make the unease in the pit of his gut lift. He made his way to the hearth where the vicar stood and gave him a nod of greeting. At least this man of God did not look at him with judgment in his eyes.

He didn't get to say anything because the door opened and Miss Clarissa appeared. She was on the arm of her uncle, but Calum did not see anyone but her.

He couldn't believe that she'd managed to look more beautiful than before. Her thick dark hair was not curled atop her head this time, most of it tumbling down her back. The length of it seemed fitting somehow. She wore a pale cream dress with layers of tulle underneath, making it slightly bigger than the other dresses he'd seen her in. The bodice clung to her nicely, however. Even from the distance, he could see the tinge of rouge on her cheeks and lips.

There was no music so when Miss Clarissa and her uncle started towards them, their movements seemed stilted. Calum did not remember to breathe until she was halfway to him. Lady Santbury melted away to the others, as did Eleanor.

"Take care of her, Your Grace," said the earl with a broad smile.

Calum only nodded. He didn't take Miss Clarissa's hand. She kept them folded in front of her as she came to his side.

"You look handsome, Your Grace," she said softly.

And you look absolutely breathtaking. He knew that he should say the words, though perhaps not as strongly as he thought it. He only turned to face the vicar instead.

If the vicar overheard their uncomfortable exchange, he made no indication. He cleared his throat and began reading from the Book of Common Prayers. Calum tuned him out. Other than his voice the room was utterly silent. It was as uncomfortable as he'd expected it to be.

For some reason, Calum glanced at Miss Clarissa. Her face was…odd. Bordering on expressionless but that wasn't really it. Expressionless was the look on Lady Quelshire's face during their dinner. Miss Clarissa seemed to be hiding what she was truly thinking behind invisible walls.

What would it be like to peer behind them, he wondered.

Calum refocused his attention on the vicar, putting that thought out of his head. He only needed to make it to the end of this. Thankfully, it seemed like the vicar was winding to a finish.

Finally, it came time for them to say their vows. They faced each other. The vicar told them what to say and they recited them. Calum in a low, uninterested tone. Clarissa with slight passion in her voice, speaking loudly and simply. Even though it was clear that they had no emotional interest in each other, he could not look away.

"You may kiss the bride."

The words shocked him so much that Calum looked sharply at the vicar. The pious man only raised his brows expectantly.

"I don't think—" Clarissa began but Calum cut her off with an annoyed hiss.

"It's fine," he grunted. "It is customary, after all."

A glimmer of surprise flashed in her eyes before Calum took a step closer. He didn't give her any chance to prepare. He didn't even give himself time to think through what he was doing. He only leaned in and pressed a kiss against her lips.

It was meant to be chaste and impersonal but it turned into something else. He didn't expect her lips to be so soft, nor the quick exhale of breath that sounded like a soft sigh. For some reason, he didn't pull away immediately. He lingered there, until she relaxed, until it felt as if she was leaning into the kiss herself.

Then he snapped back into reality. He stepped away, covering up his disconcertment with his usual glare. "Are we done?" he asked the vicar to which the man nodded.

Calum took that as his chance to turn and stalk towards the door. But Eleanor slid into his path just before he could leave. "Where do you think you are going?" she asked him, palm to his chest.

"To my chambers. We are finished here."

"We are not. There is still the wedding breakfast."

Calum blinked at her. Surely he'd misheard that. "The what?"

Lady Santbury appeared at Eleanor's side. "The wedding breakfast," she stated. "You cannot have a wedding without one. Arranged or no."

"She's right about that, Your Grace," Lord Santbury said, joining them by the door. "And you will come to learn that my wife is rarely ever wrong."

The earl patted him amicably on the shoulder and the three of them left the room. Before he could even think of a response, Louisa went by too, holding the arm of her mother. Lady Quelshire shot him a deathly glare before dabbing her eyes with her handkerchief. The vicar brushed past him as well. And at last came Miss Clarissa.

"Surely you will not be attending as well," Calum snapped at the sight of her, frustrated that this was all happening without his input.

She tilted her head, staring up at him with an impassive gaze. She looked completely unaffected by the kiss they had shared. That bothered him for some reason.

"Why would I not?" she asked him.

"This is not meant to be a joyous occasion," he reminded her. "This is a marriage of convenience."

"That does not mean we should not eat." She turned back to the door and then paused before looking over her shoulder at him. "I think it would be better if we ate together, don't you?"

His glare deepened. She blinked once.

"Perhaps not."

Then she was gone without a backward glance, leaving Calum with the uneasy feeling that he might have made a dreadful mistake.

***

By the time Calum made it to the dining room, the room was already lit with conversation. No one seemed to notice his entrance. He skulked into the room with his dour mood and settled at the head of the table yet no one spared him a glance.

Lord and Lady Santbury seemed to have endless things to talk about with Eleanor. Miss Clarissa, whom he supposed was now the Duchess of Thorneshire, sat to his left and had her head bent towards her sister as they whispered to each other. The only person who did not seem inclined to speak was Lady Olivia. She'd gone quiet again, sitting as still as a stone.

The table was laden with far too much food, Calum thought broodingly. And he was in no mood to eat. He only sat and watched and stewed as everyone enjoyed this wedding breakfast without him.

He didn't miss the way Clarissa's eyes darted to him now and again. He was tempted to do the same but was committed to his glowering, eyes burning into anyone who dared attempt to pull him into conversation. They got the hint soon enough and ignored him fully. That only worsened his mood.

By the end of it, he was ready to lash out at something. Calum held onto the reins of his irritation as best as he could when Lord Santbury stood and said, "This has been a marvelous time, but I believe it is time for us to leave the newlywed couple alone."

Calum looked over at Clarissa. If the idea of that frightened or bothered her, she made no indication. She simply stood and made her way around the table to her uncle, stepping into his arms.

"Thank you," she murmured, loud enough for Calum to hear. "For everything."

"What are families for?" the earl asked as he returned her hug. His wife came to his side and Clarissa wordlessly slipped into her arms. Calum realized with a start that they were both crying.

"I cannot believe that this is really happening." Another crying lady stepped into the fray. Miss Louisa was an open crier. As opposed to her sister's genteel weeping and delicate dabbing at her eyes, Miss Louisa's cheeks were already moist with tears and she sniffled unabashedly. "What will I do with myself now that you are gone?"

"I am not too far and you are always free to visit," Clarissa told her as she pulled her into an embrace. She met her mother's eyes, who was still seated at the table. "As are you, Mother."

Lady Quelshire stared back at her daughter, tears filling her eyes. She said nothing. As if she felt Calum's stare, her gaze turned vicious as they shot to him.

"This is a happy day," the earl spoke up. "We should not end it by crying like this. That cannot be very lucky for the new couple.'"

He kept referring to them as if this were a loving union and not a decision he'd made with obvious reluctance. Calum didn't bother to point it out. He left them be, feeling something shift within him at the obvious displays of affection. Despite how they'd acted, they were a closely knit family. And Clarissa seemed far more in touch with her emotions than he'd first thought.

"We shall visit," Lady Santbury promised. She took the hands of her niece and husband and began leading them away. Lady Quelshire silently rose and followed. "Once we're certain that the time is right."

"You may even come tomorrow if you wish," Clarissa called after. Calum noticed that she did not follow them, remaining by the table instead.

"Somehow I do not think your husband will like that," Lady Santbury said with a laugh.

Eleanor, who had been quiet while they said their goodbyes, hurried to her feet and said, "I believe that is my cue to leave as well."

"You are welcome to stay, El—" Calum began but she cut him off.

"No, no, I do not *want* to stay. I think you should spend some time alone with each other." She winked at him and Calum grimaced. "I will visit soon."

And then she was off. And they were alone.

The silence was uncomfortable. Calum knew it would be best to leave the room, to retreat to the solace of his study and blur his senses with whiskey. But he stayed seated instead, watching Clarissa as she came towards him.

"So," she said. "What do we do now?"

Calum blurted out a harsh laugh. He hadn't expected that. "You are free to do as you wish. You are now the Duchess of Thorneshire, after all."

Clarissa regarded him unblinkingly. "Then perhaps you can call me by my name. Clarissa. It would be rather odd if husband and wife spoke with such unfamiliarity, even though that is the case."

"You may do whatever you wish, as I've said." Calum scraped his chair back as he came to a stand. "I shan't stand in your way, nor do I expect you to stand in mine."

She said nothing as he stalked by. Calum felt an odd sense of relief when she finally did before he could leave. "What about my duty to you?" she asked. When he turned to frown at her, she clarified, "My duty to bear an heir for you."

Calum felt another laugh of surprise bubble up inside him and he had to exert some effort to suppress it. How could she say such a thing with such a serious countenance?

"We are in no rush," he told her.

"I see." She hesitated. "Then I shall visit your library."

"It matters not to me what you do," he said dismissively and turned to leave again. This time, she said nothing to stop him. And Calum tried not to feel disappointed in that fact.

Chapter Eight

Thorneshire Estate was not too far from her uncle's townhouse, though it stood on the outskirts of London. It would not take her too long to visit them. Clarissa consoled herself with that fact as she began to make her way through the seemingly endless hallways this manor boasted.

Her aim had been to find the library. And when she realized that she'd gotten hopelessly lost, Clarissa decided that she should simply attempt to tour the manor and get her bearings. She was the new mistress of the manor, after all. As surreal as that felt, she would have to get used to her new responsibility quickly.

By the time she saw another person, Clarissa let out a sigh of relief. She thought she would be lost forever. If she ever doubted the duke's wealth before, spending time in his manor brought her back to reality.

The woman she saw was a servant, Clarissa realized. And she was coming straight to her. She was far older, with chubby cheeks and warm eyes. She curtsied.

"Good day, Your Grace," she greeted. "It is a pleasure to meet you at last. My name is Mrs. Grace Dawson and I am the housekeeper of this manor."

"Good day, Mrs. Dawson," Clarissa greeted back. "It is nice meeting you as well. Have you been the housekeeper for long?"

"For as long as the current duke has been alive, at least," Mrs. Dawson said simply. "May I show you to your chambers?"

"Oh, certainly."

The words were hardly out of her mouth before Mrs. Dawson turned and continued back the way she'd come. Clarissa quickly fell in step behind her. She was a brisk walker, Clarissa realized.

"I'm afraid I may need a tour of the manor, Mrs. Dawson," Clarissa spoke again. "My aim was to find the library and yet I found myself hopelessly lost instead."

"That can easily be arranged, Your Grace. Would you like for me to arrange for one of the maids to do it?"

"No, I would like for you to do it, if you are not too busy."

Perhaps it was the way that Clarissa said her words but Mrs.

Dawson gave her a slightly startled look. "Me?"

"Yes. I already like you. You seem like a sound yet kind woman. It would be nice to share your company for a while." Clarissa looked away as she spoke, hoping the heat on her cheeks was not visible. Would Mrs. Dawson see right through her attempts to make a friend here?

If she did, she wouldn't know because Mrs. Dawson faced forward and continued her quick pace. "Your wish is my command, Your Grace."

Clarissa smiled privately, considering that a success. She tried not to think about the fact that Mrs. Dawson was only fulfilling a request as a servant and not because she truly wanted to.

"May I ask you a question, Mrs. Dawson?" Clarissa spoke again after a while.

"Of course, Your Grace."

"What is the duke like?"

Mrs. Dawson paused. Clarissa wondered if she was choosing her words carefully. And then she said, "His Grace is a misunderstood man. But he is kind, though stoic. And he loves deeply."

Clarissa nodded in agreement. That wasn't what she'd wanted to hear. She'd assumed as much about the duke just by observing him. What she truly wanted to know was if he harbored the temper said in the rumors. She just didn't know how to ask it.

Before she could find the right words, Mrs. Dawson stopped before a heavy, oak door. "This is the guest chambers His Grace chose for you. If it is not to your liking, you need only let me know and I shall find another for you."

"I'm sure that this is fine," Clarissa assured her.

Mrs. Dawson nodded and opened the door. Standing within with a nervous expression on her face was a maid, wiping her hands on the front of her apron. She could not have been much older than Clarissa, with sandy brown hair tucked under a cotton cap and dark brown eyes. A smattering of freckles adorned her cheeks and nose.

"This is Sarah Collins," Mrs. Dawson announced. "She will be your lady's maid going forward."

"I am pleased to meet you, Your Grace," Sarah said softly,

lowering into a curtsy.

"Likewise, Sarah. Have you been here long?"

Sarah's eyes darted up to her with uncertainty. "I have been in the duke's employment for a few months now."

"That is nice. We are both new then." Clarissa offered her a smile but it didn't seem to ease the other girl's anxiousness. She supposed her second attempt at making a friend here was falling flat once again.

A hesitant smile flashed across Sarah's face. Mrs. Dawson spoke again. "I shall take my leave now, Your Grace. Please let me know if there is anything you may need."

"I shall," Clarissa managed to say before Mrs. Dawson turned and exited the room.

Slowly, Clarissa faced what was now her new bedchamber. It was opulent with a large mahogany bed occupying the north of the room. At the other end stood a hearth, a fire already glowing within, a fancy chamber pot on one side and a desk and chair on the other. She had a vanity table and a dresser standing next to a door she suspected might be a closet room. It was far bigger than her room had been at Quelshire Manor and certainly more personal than her room at her uncle's. There was even a stack of paper and an inkpot on the desk.

Clarissa wandered over to it, a soft smile touching her lips. Had the duke put this here knowing that she was fond of writing poems? It felt odd making such an assumption about a man she hardly knew, a man everyone claimed was a monster, and yet it also felt fitting.

"Do you need assistance with changing out of your dress, Your Grace?" Sarah spoke up, cutting through Clarissa's thoughts.

"Yes, thank you," Clarissa breathed. She went to the center of the room, standing still as Sarah began undoing the laces on the back of her dress. The silence that ensued quickly grew uncomfortable. Clarissa racked her brain for something to say.

"Do you like it here, Sarah?" she asked.

Sarah jolted, like she didn't expect to be spoken to. "Y-yes, Your Grace."

"What do you like most about it?" she asked, hoping her voice was gentle enough to put her maid at ease.

"I am not sure, Your Grace," Sarah answered softly.

Clarissa thinned her lips. She was accustomed to silence, enjoying it thoroughly whenever she was alone. But now that everything was said and done, her family in London while she was here in an unfamiliar place, she craved something to latch on to. Clarissa knew that she could write to Louisa and the others whenever she wanted to. But visiting them was no longer as easy as going down the hallway, or seeking them in one of the parlors.

She felt…lonely.

The unwelcoming duke did not make it any better. It suddenly occurred to Clarissa that she was in this massive manor and she was utterly alone.

Perhaps it was because she already missed her family but the thought tightened her throat with hidden tears. Still, she could not find the right words to say. Sarah assisted her out of the dress and into a far more humble piece, which took the better part of an hour. Clarissa made more attempts at conversation but, perhaps it was because she was the new mistress of this household, that Sarah's responses were simple. It was like pulling water out of stone.

"Thank you, Sarah," Clarissa said when she was done. "Before you leave, may I trouble you with something else?"

"Yes, Your Grace," Sarah responded without hesitation.

"Could you show me to the library?"

Sarah nodded and led the way out of the bedchamber. Clarissa resigned herself to a quiet trip. At least if she could not befriend the help, she could bury her nose in a book and wait until she was called upon by the duke.

Which she would inevitably be if his plans were to believed.

Clarissa ignored the tremor of trepidation she felt at the thought of sharing the duke's bed. Hopefully she would not have to worry about that for some time to come.

Sarah drew to a sudden halt, pulling Clarissa from her thoughts. Only then did she realize that there was someone standing just a few feet away from them. A lanky man wearing large spectacles gave them a long, hard stare.

"M-Mr. Huntington," Sarah stammered, sinking into a bow.

The man did not spare Sarah a glance. His attention rested solely on Clarissa. As he drew closer, Clarissa saw stony eyes behind the frames of his spectacles.

"Who are you?"

His voice was firm and commanding. He was clearly a man of power since Sarah was all but trembling next to her. Clarissa met his gaze, considering the best way to respond. She decided on something simple. "My name is Clarissa."

"Clarissa." Her name rolled off his tongue, sending a shiver down her spine. "The eldest daughter of the Baron of Quelshire. Niece to the Earl of Santbury. What are you doing here, Clarissa?"

Clarissa tried not to feel bothered by the way he listed out her relations. He was scrutinizing her, she realized. His gaze ran down the length of her and back up to her face, narrowing as if he was not pleased with what he saw.

"If you know me so well, Mr. Huntington, I would think that you'd already know the answer to your question. Who are you, good sir?"

Mr. Huntington raised his chin. "I am Mr. Stephen Huntington, the duke's steward and his closest relative."

"Then it is a pleasure meeting you, Mr. Huntington." Clarissa dutifully curtsied. "His Grace did not speak about you. I was not aware that he had any other close relatives, beside Lady Yulebridge."

His nose slightly wrinkled. "You have not answered my question. What are you doing here?"

Was that hostility she detected in his tone? What could she have done to upset this man already? Clarissa held his stare, thinking back on all her interactions with the duke and his aunt. Neither had ever made mention of this man so surely she could not have said or done anything offensive, could she?

"I am the new Duchess of Thorneshire."

Saying it aloud felt surreal. Astonishment overtook the gentleman's countenance before it transformed into a stern expression. It was evident that he was displeased by her confession, yet she was too overwhelmed by her own emotions to pay much heed to his reaction.

She was a duchess. A wealthy one, by anyone's measure. Her world had laid crumbled at her feet for so long that she could hardly believe a new one had built up around her so quickly. The walls were taller, reinforced, and she stood queen.

"I see." Stephen Huntington pushed his spectacles up his

nose. "I see much has happened while I was away. Perhaps I should have returned sooner."

"Yes, perhaps. We could have met at an earlier date."

"Hm." Stephen did not say anything before stalking by her. Clarissa blinked, shocked by the sheer rudeness of his dismissal. After a moment, she turned and watched his retreat but he was already turning the corner onto another hallway.

Annoyance filtered through her. Clarissa drew in a deep breath, letting it out her nose silently. It didn't abate the feeling but at least she could shove it behind her mask before she faced Sarah.

"Shall we?" she said to her. Sarah nodded eagerly, clearly not as skilled at masking her fright as Clarissa was masking everything else. Together, the continued on their way as Clarissa tried her best to forget about her unsavory introduction to the duke's steward.

Chapter Nine

This nightmare was particularly vicious.

It always started out the same, with Violet accusing him of not saving her in time. It always ended the same as well, Calum on his knees, tears on his face as he begged for her forgiveness.

Compared to the others, there weren't many differences with this one. Yet it left him utterly derailed. He shot upright in bed with his breath lodged firmly in his throat and his hair plastered to his face. He decided to sleep without a shirt, knowing that he would only wake in a pool of his own sweat and he felt an instant rush of cool air as he swung out of bed. His legs were unsteady, heart beating so madly that he was truly afraid it would tear right out of his chest.

He couldn't handle this any longer.

The guilt was all consuming. It ate him from within, chipping away what was left of his sanity. Calum struggled to make it to the other end of the room where his chamber pot stood before he emptied the contents of his stomach. Marvelous. Now he would have to keep it at his bedside while he slept.

He heaved until he could not any longer. Violet's death had not been particularly bloody this time. It was her words that had done him in.

You did this.

How could you let this happen to me?

I hate you I hate you I hate you I hate you

He could still hear her voice echoing in his head. While alive, those words had never passed her lips. Calum didn't think Violet capable of hating anyone. But in death, her hatred ran so deep that he felt it touch his soul. It also elicited a certain sentiment within him, one that he struggled to articulate but sensed that Violet was attempting to convey a message to him.

He sank onto the floor, putting his back against the cool wall. He watched as the room grew brighter as time slipped away from him. It must have been a little before dawn when he woke. Any time now, his valet will come walking through those doors with fear in his eyes and shaking hands.

Calum didn't want to have to deal with that right now. He

dragged himself to a stand, swaying on his feet. Maybe he should have eaten something before retiring to bed last night. He'd stayed holed up in his study all night until he'd drunken himself into a stupor before dragging himself to his chambers. His stomach had grumbled in protest last night and right now it roared.

Still, he somehow managed to change out of the rest of his sweat-sodden clothes and into something fresher. He left his bedchamber quickly, not wanting to run into his valet or Mrs. Dawson or anyone else.

As quickly as he could, he sought the reclusion of his study. Calum drew to a halt when he saw Stephen already seated within.

"What are you doing here?" Calum blurted out.

Stephen was reading something, his spectacles perched on the very tip of his nose. He pushed it back up as he looked at Calum. "I returned yesterday afternoon."

"And you said nothing to me?"

"You were too busy partaking in a lovely session of drinking and mourning," Stephen drawled, returning his attention to his book.

Calum frowned. Stephen wasn't this early of a riser. Yet it seemed as if he had been here long before Calum. "I thought you were meant to return later today."

"That was the plan, but my meetings ended earlier than I had expected them to." Stephen flipped a page. He didn't speak again until Calum had crossed over to his desk. "I have met your wife."

Calum halted. Stephen spoke simply but he knew better than to think he wasn't disappointed.

"I ran into her in the west wing," Stephen went on. "And she boldly told me that she is the new Duchess of Thorneshire. A brazen little thing she is. She must have been waiting for this her entire life."

"I know that this is not what you wanted—" Calum began.

"This is the exact opposite of what I wanted," Stephen cut in.

"But that matters not now," Calum stated firmly. A megrim was already poking holes into his temple. He eyed his decanter of brandy. "What is done is done and I do not regret my decision."

Stephen sighed heavily. All of a sudden, the façade he had been painting tore in two. He set the book down and was on his feet in a second.

"Surely I have explained to you the consequences of making such a decision?" Stephen said, pacing back and forth.

"Do not speak to me as if I am a child, Stephen," Calum snapped. He ignored the brandy that was beckoning to him. "I know more than anyone else what everyone thinks of me. But that does not mean I do not have a duty. Clarissa was the only lady who seemed not to care about the rumours."

"And you do not find that odd?" At Calum's incredulous look, Stephen let out a breath of frustration. "They believe what they wish to believe and no one takes a chance to learn the truth, Calum. What makes Miss Clarissa any different? Are you sure that she is not just after you for your wealth?"

"She is not," Calum said with an odd sense of certainty he didn't know he possessed. "And even if she was, it does not matter. Half of the ton are after the same thing, just in different people."

Stephen sighed, pinching the bridge of his nose. He seemed well and truly distressed. "I am just concerned that this may end up doing more harm than good."

Calum leaned over his desk, interlacing his fingers. "You say that you have met her?"

"Yes. Briefly."

"And what do you think?"

Stephen frowned, as if the question threw him. It threw Calum as well. He didn't know why he cared enough to ask it but it was already out there.

"She seems…blunt."

A huff of a chuckle escaped Calum's lips. Finally unable to help himself, he made for his brandy. "That is certainly one way of describing her."

He poured himself a glass and the first sip instantly calmed his still frazzled nerves. Calum didn't realize that Stephen was still staring at him with that frown on his face until he turned back to meet him.

"I do not care about her any more than she cares about me," Calum said gruffly. "She is only a means to an end, nothing more. As you get to know her yourself, you will see that she is not so bad. She likes…poetry."

Stephen only stared at him as if he'd grown a second head. Calum couldn't hold his gaze for long. He already felt out of it since waking this morning. This conversation about Clarissa was not making him feel any more settled.

"Then, if we are done here." Calum finished his drink and made for the door.

"Where are you going?" Stephen asked.

"Away from here," Calum stated. He didn't realize how odd it sounded for someone like him until he was already stalking down the hallway.

***

"I have been looking for you."

Calum sighed softly, not turning at the voice. Mrs. Dawson had quite the knack for finding him when he didn't want to be found.

He'd left for the gardens of all places because no one would expect him to be there. A few hours of silence and solitude was all he needed and he could no longer find it in his study. Not with Stephen there questioning his decisions.

But he should have known that it would not be so easy.

She came to his side, sitting on the bench he occupied. They were under one of the three gazebos in his gardens. Violet had loved reading in the gazebo but not the one he sat under today. That one was in a section of the garden he no longer visited.

"Is something bothering you, Your Grace?" Mrs. Dawson asked after a while.

Calum tried not to sigh. "Why have you sought me out, Mrs. Dawson?"

"I wished to know if you intend to have breakfast. I brought your tray to your study but you were not there. Then I grew worried."

"I am a grown man. I can take care of myself."

He felt her looking at him from the corner of his eye. Calum realized a moment too late that his words had come out a bit too bitter. He didn't try to take them back though. Bitterness was mild to the other emotions that plagued him and he was sure that Mrs. Dawson knew it well too.

"That is true," she said after a moment. "And I suppose you have a wife who will be able to take care of you as well."

Calum barked a harsh laugh. "You are a smarter woman than that, Mrs. Dawson. You know better than to think that our marriage is anything but one of convenience."

"That does not mean you cannot share in each other's company. It is an easy solution for two lonely people."

"Clarissa is far from lonely. She has a family that loves her and waits just a few hours away for their chance to visit."

"You believe that she is not lonely, Your Grace?" Mrs. Dawson asked in the tone of a gentle schoolteacher. As if she was trying to give him the chance to reconsider his response. Calum didn't rise to her bait and she sighed. "If that is what you wish to believe, Your Grace. Will you be having breakfast in your study or your chambers? Or perhaps will you break your fast with your new wife in the breakfast parlour?"

"She is already awake?" Calum asked in surprise. It was still quite early.

"She has been for a while now and has been spending her morning in the library."

"Hm," was all he could think to say now that his mind was filled with thoughts of Clarissa. He could see her now, sitting with her back straight and her hair piled atop her head under a particularly golden ray of sunlight. She must read like she did everything else. With precise perfection.

"Breakfast, Your Grace?" Mrs. Dawson called again, dragging him from his thoughts.

"What? Oh, no, I don't want anything."

"You should eat, Your Grace," Mrs. Dawson insisted gently and to that he only steeled his eyes, giving her a faint glare. She nodded in understanding even though she didn't bother to hide her disappointment. "I understand."

Calum didn't listen to her retreat. His mind had wandered back to Clarissa, the dregs of his nightmare fading to pieces in the back of his mind. She liked to read, he reminded himself. She'd said so herself. If he were to follow Mrs. Dawson's not-so-subtle advice to give her company, wouldn't he only disturb her?

The more he thought about it, the more certain he felt that he would be. Despite that, he stood. He left the gardens and took long, healthy strides to the library, not allowing himself to consider what he was doing. Only when he came upon the door did he stop in his tracks and really thought about what he was about to do.

Calum gritted his teeth, annoyed that he'd allowed himself to come here in the first place.

But then his ears pricked at an odd sound. It was a little off-kilter, like it was meant to be a soft tune but cracked at the very end. There was a short pause and for a moment, Calum thought he might have imagined it.

But then the sound returned, louder than before. It was singing he realized. Horrible singing of a song he did not know but singing nonetheless.

His actions were not entirely his own when he opened the library door. Like a helpless man drawn by the call of a siren—albeit a bad one—he could not stop himself.

Clarissa stood within, her back turned to him. Calum felt oddly like a man in a trance as he watched her reach up on her toes to pull something from the bookshelf. She continued to sing with abandon and even laughed softly to herself when she cracked, only to continue again. She remained unaware of him the entire time, even when she turned to his direction and made her way to the settee.

She did not look at all the way he'd imagined. Somehow, she managed to exceed his expectations. She did not sit with her back and legs straight but twisted slightly with her legs tucked beneath her. Her hair was down her back, a few of the pieces around her face tucked to the nape of her neck. She didn't stop singing as she opened her book and somehow, the off-tune sound of it did not grate on his nerves the way that it should have.

He could not move, could not breathe. Calum was trapped, realizing a little too late that the sight of her pulled on something long buried within him. Something he desperately needed to keep trapped under everything else.

Chapter Ten

"What are you doing?" Calum asked, surprising Clarissa.

Clarissa yelped with such force she nearly vaulted out of her seat. Her book, however, did not fare much better. It thudded to the floor but the sound fell on deaf ears as she took in her husband's aloof gaze.

Her husband...

It still hadn't sunken in yet. And looking at him now only made this entire situation harder to believe. Bathed in the morning light sifting through the library windows, she saw no hint of the monster they spoke of. Rather, she saw nothing but a chiseled face, deep-set eyes, and a hard mouth. She was struck once more by the thought that he was so devastatingly handsome that it emptied her mind of proper thoughts.

But then his words registered and she blinked. "I am singing. Was it not obvious?"

He blinked and for a brief moment, she saw a shadow of surprise in his eyes. They appeared darker than usual right now, as if the shadows that constantly lurked there were rearing their heads.

"Forgive my surprise at what you call singing," he said.

Clarissa only stared at him. She didn't even pick up the book that had slipped from her lap. An uncomfortable quiet stretched between them but neither one of them looked away.

At last, she asked, "Did you come here to comment on my horrible singing?"

"No, I did not."

Again, there was silence. Clarissa frowned a little. Trying to get a proper response from him was like forcing a dry river to spring water.

"Well, if you have nothing more to say..." Clarissa reached for her book. She tried to keep her attention on the words again but her husband lingering at the doorway made it difficult.

She listened to the creak of the floorboards as he delved further into the room. The door clicked shut behind him and, all of a sudden, Clarissa couldn't breathe. Every nerve in her body came to attention as he wandered close enough for her to smell him. He smelled like...flowers? And something else. Spicy and strong, just a wisp of it before it was gone.

Curious, she peeked up at him from beneath her lashes. He didn't seem to know what to do with himself. He ran his fingers along the end of the bookshelf. He pulled one free and skimmed through the pages before resting it on a table nearby. After a while, Clarissa could not help but look up at him directly, watching as he meandered over to the hearth and fiddled with the poker.

"Is there something you would like to say, Calum?"

His name on her lips must have startled him. At least, that was what she thought she saw when he looked at her. If it was, it was gone in a flash.

"No, I have nothing to say to you."

"Then why do you amble about as if you would like to say something but do not know how to?" she inquired.

His brows dipped slightly. "It is my manor. I am allowed to go and come as I please."

"That is certainly true," she conceded. "Forgive me then. I did not mean to be rude."

Calum nodded and looked away. To the ceiling, across the room, at the floor. Clarissa felt a smile tug at her lips.

"Would you like to sit with me?"

Again, he seemed surprised. Clarissa was almost certain that he would deny her and she braced herself for the blow of rejection. But then, stiffly, he made his way over to the settee she occupied and sat.

There was considerable distance between them and yet her hair stood on end, her heart fluttering when he met her eyes.

"I do not mean to interrupt you," he said in such a low tone that she had to stare at his lips to hear him. "I only...wanted to see if you were faring well. Settling in, I mean."

The question touched her. She was certain he hadn't cared about such things. "I have. Everyone has been kind to me. Well, almost everyone."

"You mean, Stephen."

It wasn't a question. "He does not appear to be pleased with our marriage. I may even go as far as to say that he did not know you planned on getting married at all."

"He means well," Calum responded, rubbing his jaw.

"I'm sure that he does. And I am a stranger to him. Perhaps he only needs time to grow accustomed to me."

"Perhaps," he murmured and there was something in the way he said it that made her doubt if it was true.

Again the scent of him wafted over to her. This time she recognized the harsh scent. "Have you been drinking, Calum?"

His eyes narrowed. "I have. What of it?"

"It is rather early."

"That matters not to me. Is it not my free will that allows me to do things when I want?"

"Undoubtedly," she answered without hesitation. "But one would think that society's expectations of us force us to act in limiting manners."

"I care not about what society thinks."

"That much is clear to me." Realizing a beat later how her words could be misconstrued, Clarissa lifted her lips into a smile. "But I think that is an admirable trait. One I wish I could emulate one day."

His frown deepened again, but it wasn't out of his usual irritation. He seemed confused. "Are you always like this?"

Clarissa blinked. "Like what?"

"So candid. So…bare."

A surprised chuckle blurted from her lips. "Does it bother you, Calum? If it does, I assure you that you will not be the first. Many others find my demeanour off-putting."

"Is that what they have told you?"

"Many in less kinder words." The look on his face made her laugh again. "I don't mean to incite your pity. It is simply the truth. And I have a few friends who do not mind how serious I can be."

Well, one, she thought. *And Louisa. So, two.*

Still, Calum regarded her as if she were an unusual creature that he was trying to understand. Clarissa couldn't help doing the same. He'd come to seek her out, she realized, even though he did not want to admit it. And now he was sitting with her, engaging in conversation.

He was lonely.

It was written deep into his bones, carved from his flesh. The layers of defensive walls he put up around him could not stop the ache of his loneliness from showing.

For a brief, fearful moment, Clarissa was tempted to reach out and take his hand. She didn't dare, turning her attention to her book instead.

"You have a wonderful collection, by the way. I have not read this one in quite some time." She studied his face, perhaps a little more keenly than she needed to. He was too handsome not to stare at, after all. "And judging by the look on your face, you have not either."

"You're right. I haven't seen it in some time. It was my mother's."

The confession surprised her. His attention remained on the book in her lap, his gaze far away. "It is well loved," she commented softly. "It must have been her favourite."

"It was. Her influence led me to love poetry as well."

"Would you care to read me one of her preferred poems?" she asked tentatively.

Calum's eyes snapped to hers. The intensity of his gaze sent a shiver down her spine. She searched his eyes and felt something shift between them as if the walls were beginning to crumble.

This time she was certain that he would deny her. She was honestly surprised that he had decided to stay this long.

So she couldn't think of a single thing to say or do when he reached forward and took the book from her. Their fingers brushed, the brief contact enough to steal her breath away. At this rate, she was bound to start wheezing.

Clarissa schooled her expression as best as she could but she doubted it worked. He must have noticed the blush now staining her cheeks, her face so hot that it warmed her entire body. And even if he hadn't, surely he could hear the rapid pound of her heart against her ribcage?

If he did, he ignored it. His attention was on the book, holding it reverently in both hands. "I did not think I would ever touch this book again," he murmured, perhaps to himself. But Clarissa heard him. And the small confession touched her in ways she couldn't understand.

Clarissa watched with bated breath as he skipped a few pages. He finally came to a stop and Clarissa braced herself.

Before he could begin, there was a sharp knock on the door. Whoever it was didn't bother to wait for a response before opening the door. Clarissa felt a sharp stab of disappointment when she saw Stephen's tight, frustrated expression.

"Pardon the intrusion, Calum" he clipped. "But there are urgent business matters that require your immediate attention."

"You can take care of it," Calum said dismissively, already scowling.

"Unfortunately, I cannot." Stephen's eyes darted to Clarissa. "Please excuse us, Your Grace."

Clarissa nodded. She felt a pang of dismay when Calum got to a stand, his scowl now out with full force. He held the book oddly in his hand as he said, "Another time then."

"Another time," Clarissa murmured and watched as they both left the room.

She didn't reach for the book of poetry until long after he was gone. Even then, she could hardly see any of the words. It felt as if she'd nearly broken through the layers of ice above her head but she was still drowning. He'd seemed different than all the other times they'd interacted. Human. A man with a soul far too big for his body.

Clarissa had gotten a peep of who he was and now she was yearning for more.

***

"If this is a waste of my time, then you will surely regret it."

"I, for one, thought that you would be glad to leave," Stephen responded in a drawl.

Calum gritted his teeth. He strode into his study at such a brisk pace that he was a little alarmed at how easily Stephen followed. He didn't bother to grace that with a response. Mostly because he didn't really have one. He wasn't entirely certain why he'd stayed there so long in the first place.

He blamed it on the strength of his nightmare earlier this morning. Perhaps he was feeling sentimental, a weakness that had not plagued him in years. That was the only reason he could think.

"Out with it," he snapped, marching over to his sideboard. Clarissa's words whispered through his mind and he hesitated.

"Calum?" Stephen called from behind.

Calum bit back a curse. His cousin had always been adept at

seeing what Calum didn't want him to see. Calum made his way to his desk instead, hoping that Stephen wouldn't comment on his odd behavior.

He didn't, but his slight frown deepened. "I have reports," he began, "of several tenants withholding their rental payments. Apparently, they are disgruntled because of overdue repairs."

"Waste of my time," Calum growled, his irritation evident in the sharpness of his tone. "And you called me here for this? Why do I have you as my steward if not to handle such affairs in my stead? Meet with these upset tenants and begin negotiations!"

Stephen flinched. The sight rocked Calum back into reality.

The monster had reared its ugly head again.

As swiftly as his anger came, it dissolved to leave nothing but shame. Calum shot out of his chair, stalking over to the closest window, upset with himself for his bad temper. Again, he'd spoken too harshly. Of course, others were bound to call him a beast when he acted like this.

An apology stuck in his throat. Behind him, Stephen cleared his throat.

"With respect, Calum, I urge you to do so instead. They will not want to hear from me."

"And what makes you think they would rather want to speak to me? You know what their opinion of me is."

"Then when you do, face their complaints head on or they will see it as a sign of weakness."

Calum turned to look at him, meeting Stephen's steady stare. His meaning was clear. *Don't get too angry or it will only make things worse.*

He let his breath out through his nose, slowly calming his rising temper. Stephen was right. And if he continued like this, he was only bound to exacerbate the already terrible reputation. Preserving his father's legacy did not simply end with providing an heir, he knew.

Still, nothing but apprehension whispered through him at the thought of doing any of his ducal duties. He'd left it in Stephen's hands for so long that he couldn't remember half of the things he had to do. All he'd done was dig himself into a deep hole so the light peeping in from above only stung his eyes.

"Very well," Calum clipped. "Is that all?"

"I have left the reports on your desk," Stephen said calmly. "Just in case you wish to look through them before you decide to meet them."

All Calum could manage was a grunt. Stephen seemed to take that as a confirmation because he said, "I shall leave you be then."

He listened as Stephen left. Then he stalked over to the sideboard, unable to help himself any longer. This brandy would dull his mind and leave behind the tumultuous thoughts plaguing him. Clarissa. The tenants. His temper. And as always, Violet.

She was never far from his mind. But he realized as he settled into his chair with his full glass of brandy, that she'd been further than usual. Like she had been replaced by a pair of hazel eyes instead.

Chapter Eleven

Clarissa hadn't seen Calum in days. She would be lying to herself if she claimed she wasn't disappointed.

Their brief time together in the library had only stoked her longing to learn who the duke truly was. Not the monster he tried to present as but the vulnerable man underneath. After a while, she could even admit to herself that she was a little saddened that he hadn't gotten to read for her. She'd hoped that he would seek her out another time, to finish what they had almost started.

No such luck. He stayed in either his study or his bedchamber, which Clarissa quickly learned from Sarah was off-limits to only a select few people. They were yet to share a single meal and eventually, Clarissa resigned herself to eating in her room instead. The dining room was simply far too big for just her.

Maybe she had imagined the tender moments they'd shared. Perhaps he truly had no interest in her like she'd thought.

The idea made her grimace. She wiped the look off her face quickly when there was a knock on the door of her chambers.

"Good morning, Your Grace," Mrs. Dawson greeted as she entered and curtsied.

"Oh, good morning, Mrs. Dawson," Clarissa answered in surprise. She set down the book she'd begun reading after Sarah left. "Have you always been such an early riser?"

"I have grown to become one, Your Grace," the housekeeper said. "I have come to see if you would like to continue our tour before breakfast. We could address the east wing today."

"Thank you, I would like that." Clarissa stood, setting her book aside. She followed Mrs. Dawson out of the room and managed to bite her tongue for a few minutes before she asked, "Is the Duke all right?"

Mrs. Dawson's passive expression did not move. "What do you mean, Your Grace?"

"He has been locked away in his study and chambers for some days now. And I do recall him being pulled into an urgent meeting by Mr. Huntington. I thought that perhaps something bad might have happened?"

It occurred to Clarissa suddenly that Mrs. Dawson might

have been the wrong person to ask when the housekeeper said, "I am not privy to the details of His Grace's business affairs, Your Grace."

"That's right," Clarissa mumbled, feeling a little embarrassed. "I do not know why I asked."

Mrs. Dawson brought her to the east wing within a matter of minutes. Her fast pace slowed as she began showing her the rooms located there. They were quite similar to the west wing, though there was a considerable decline in guest bedchambers.

By the end of it, they were ready to head down to the first floor. But then Clarissa noticed that there was a short hallway they had not delved down.

"What is down there?" she asked, coming to a stop.

Mrs. Dawson turned in the direction Clarissa pointed. Clarissa watched as the other woman carefully arranged her face into utter stillness.

"I do not know, Your Grace. No one is allowed to enter."

She was lying. Clarissa didn't see it in her expression rather than the lack thereof. Mrs. Dawson was hiding something.

Clarissa gazed down the hallway. It looked like any other, though it only boasted one door directly ahead of her. The walls were bare, the drapes drawn, and a dark shadow was cast over the burgundy wood.

"Something tells me you will not tell me why," Clarissa mused aloud, "even if I ask."

"It would be better to ask His Grace about it if you are curious, Your Grace."

Clarissa smiled a little. "You and I both know that he will not answer me. He is a mysterious man and is determined to remain that way."

"Perhaps. But perhaps not. You seem to have already made quite an impact on him already."

Clarissa raised her brow at Mrs. Dawson's tone. "Truly? In what way?"

"Subtle, barely noticeable ways," Mrs. Dawson said. "Ways that would be too difficult to explain. But it brings me hope that His Grace will become like his former self in time."

"And what was his former self like?" Clarissa asked, her voice tinged with eagerness.

The sides of Mrs. Dawson's lips twitched into a half-smile. "For one, Your Grace, he was as avid a reader as yourself. He would always have his nose in a book, no matter what it was about. Ever since his youth."

"Is that so?"

"It would be wonderful if he found his joy in reading again. But I know very well that these things cannot be rushed."

Clarissa could easily imagine a younger Calum reading from dusk to dawn, straining his eyes at candlelight. Seeing it in her mind's eye made her smile widen.

Before she could ask any more questions, they were interrupted by a maid. "Pardon me, Mrs. Dawson," the girl said. "His Grace is asking for his breakfast."

"Is he in the dining room?" Clarissa asked. "Or the breakfast parlour?"

The maid blinked, shaking her head. "Neither, Your Grace."

Disappointment sagged her shoulders. Mrs. Dawson noticed it and offered her a wider smile. "In time, Your Grace," she said gently.

Clarissa didn't know how long 'in time' would be. She'd never been an impatient person. But the more she learned about Calum, the more determined she became. And her determination was far more vicious than her patience.

"Please excuse me, Your Grace," Mrs. Dawson said with a slight curtsy. Then she turned back to the maid, "Hannah, please escort Her Grace to her chambers."

"No, that's fine," Clarissa quickly said. "I'm certain that I know my way back."

"As you wish, Your Grace."

And she was off without a moment of hesitation, on her way to serve her master. Clarissa watched her retreat for a brief moment and felt an odd prick of jealousy.

With a sigh, she headed back to her chambers and tried not to lament the fact that she would once again be eating alone.

***

"What took you so long?"

To his frustration, Calum sounded far more annoyed than he

felt. Mrs. Dawson's patient expression however did not move as she rested his breakfast on the desk in front of him.

"I was giving Her Grace the last of her tour," Mrs. Dawson said.

The mention of Clarissa made his heart skip a beat. To be honest, he had not been able to stop thinking about her ever since he left the office a few days ago. But every time she crossed his mind, he felt such a sharp stab of guilt that he forced himself away from any company. If Stephen came by, Calum chased him away. If his solitude felt overwhelming, he drank himself to sleep to keep from seeking Clarissa out. It was a vicious cycle that he was quickly growing tired of.

"She wanted it to be done in parts," Mrs. Dawson went on, hovering next to the desk. "According to her, if she were to be given a tour of the manor all at once, she would only forget half of it. She says we need to act efficiently. Isn't that interesting?"

Truthfully, yes. Calum was already starting to see that he found many things about Clarissa interesting. But he knew what Mrs. Dawson was doing so he said nothing, eating instead.

"She is currently having her breakfast in her chambers," Mrs. Dawson said. "And you are having yours here in your study."

"How astute of you, Mrs. Dawson," Calum drawled sarcastically.

"Wouldn't the food taste far better if consumed in the company of another?"

"If that is the case, you can have a seat while I finish my meal."

Mrs. Dawson looked dreadfully unamused. "I am busy, Your Grace."

"What a shame. A next time then."

She shook her head at him and, for a brief moment, he considered his deflection a success. But he should have known that she would not be so easily deterred.

"Do you remember how you would follow me to the kitchen when you were younger and watch me while I cook?"

Calum eyed her warily, reaching for his coffee. After one sip, he felt normal enough to last a few more hours before his constant exhaustion caught up to him again. "Vaguely."

"Well, I think about that time quite often. You'd always been the curious sort and would often seek to answer your curiosity without hesitation. Perhaps that is why I took such a liking to you."

Calum snorted, rolling his eyes. "You speak as if you had a choice. I was loved by all back then."

Mrs. Dawson laughed. It had been so long since he'd last heard it that it took him by surprise. "I cannot deny it. It makes me wish for signs of that boy again."

"He is long gone, Mrs. Dawson. I've grown out of such behaviours."

"On the contrary, I think you only grew to be a calmer, more charming version of who you were as a child. But I have not seen that side of you in a long while."

Calum met her eyes. His heart twisted in his chest to see the sadness shining in Mrs. Dawson's gaze. It was his fault. She looked at him like that because she was mourning the man he once was.

But that man could not be revived. Not while Violet still lay cold in the ground.

"Thank you for the meal, Mrs. Dawson," Calum said softly, his tone firm.

She nodded, understanding the subtle dismissal. "You are welcome, Your Grace." Then she made for the door. Calum thought that he would be saved from any more shame-inducing memories but then she paused at the threshold.

"She eats with her lady's maid."

Calum frowned at her. "Pardon me?"

"Her Grace. She has all her meals in the company of her lady's maid. I do not think she enjoys eating alone."

And then she left, her last words hanging in the air.

Chapter Twelve

"He's what?"

Sarah blinked, looking like a frightened doe. Clarissa quickly replaced her stunned look with a simple one of confusion. "Forgive me, I think I might have misheard you. Calum has asked what of me?"

"He wishes to have your company during dinner, Your Grace," Sarah said tentatively. She put her hands behind her and Clarissa instantly knew that she was rubbing her fingers together in a trepidant manner. Her lady's maid's anxiousness knew no bounds and it didn't help when Clarissa spoke so sharply to her.

"Oh," Clarissa breathed. She turned her attention to the mirror of her vanity table, staring blankly at herself. "I thought I must have been mistaken. And I assume that you do not know why?"

"I do not, Your Grace."

"Very well then. We should not keep him waiting." She picked up her brush and began running it through her hair.

"Your Grace, allow me!" Sarah rushed to her side, gently taking the brush from Clarissa's hands. Clarissa hardly noticed it.

He wanted to dine with her. Clearly something must have happened. Why else would Calum suddenly wish to share in her company when he'd shown little indication that he cared before?

Surely...surely he wasn't thinking about her as much as she thought about him?

She dismissed the thought immediately but it didn't stop the flush of heat that rushed to her cheeks. She'd resigned herself to eating with Sarah again. Sarah was afraid of her, not because of how Clarissa treated her—which Clarissa believed was rather kindly—but because of the titles that separated them. Clarissa hoped that eventually Sarah would warm up to her, but for now, they either sat in silence or Clarissa took charge of a one-sided conversation that went nowhere.

Calum on the other hand...

Her heart thumped at the thought of seeing him again. As time wore on, her impatience grew, wanting Sarah to be done with styling her hair. The quicker she finished, the quicker Clarissa could get to the dining room.

At last, she was done. Clarissa quickly left her room and headed to the dining room where Sarah said Calum waited.

And wait he did, in the most attractive manner a man could possibly do so.

It was hard reconciling the alleged beast with the duke sitting at the head of the table. He didn't know that she'd arrived. His attention was on his glass of red wine—which was half empty—with a mournful look in his eyes. It was so heart-wrenching, so devastatingly morose that tears sprang to her eyes.

But then he noticed her lingering by the doorway and that fragile look disappeared. "Aren't you going to sit?" he asked gruffly.

Clarissa swallowed past her dry throat. She hoped he could see how nervous she was now that she was here. She made her way to the chair to the left of him and sat. As soon as she did, two footmen entered the room bearing their first course.

Clarissa stole secret glances at him while their food was being served. In the time that it took for the footmen to retreat, he'd already drained his glass of wine and gotten another.

"Thank you, Calum," she said softly once they were alone again.

His eyes shot to her. He always looked a little surprised when she called him by his given name. "For what?"

"For asking me to have dinner with you."

Calum cleared his throat. "Yes, well, my housekeeper made quite a point of telling me that you might be lonely."

Clarissa blinked. "How odd. And you cared?"

"Why would I not?"

"Because you have not seemed to care about anything else that concerns me. I mean that with no bitterness, Calum. But this is a marriage of convenience so I'm sure you must have no reason to treat me kindly."

"I should not have a reason to treat you kindly," he grumbled and those words warmed her so soundly that she couldn't think of a proper response. Thankfully, he went on, "You must truly think me to be the monster that they say I am, if this is enough to take you by surprise."

"It was not the rumours that caused my assumptions but

simply all our conversations," she said simply, recovering. "Though I do think we had a lovely discussion in the library a few days ago."

"Enough of this talk. Eat."

Calum drained his glass again and signaled for another. While the footman poured him another glass, Clarissa watched as Calum took a bite of his food. She knew she seemed odd, staring at him like she was. But she couldn't help herself. And when he caught her eyes with a frown, she smiled.

"What is it?" he demanded to know.

"You are eating," she commented.

His frown only deepened. He looked at his plate, then back at her. "Is that so unusual?"

"It should not be. But this is my first time seeing you eat like a man with a hearty appetite. You tend to pick at your food."

This time when he scowled at her, Clarissa felt no apprehension. She only laughed, amusement tickling her. "You pay far too much attention to me, Clarissa."

There it was.

She tried not to react but the sound of her name made her stomach twist, heat spreading through her chest. It was silly, she knew. Utterly childish. And yet her smile widened.

"I cannot deny it," she said past her grin. "But can you help me? You are an odd man."

"Some may call that off-putting."

"That is fine. I am used to off-putting."

The wrinkle of his scowl smoothed away. Something passed behind his eyes. Calum only stared at her for a few seconds and Clarissa found herself trapped beneath the weight of his gaze. She thought he might say something, that he might reveal another part of himself that would draw her further in his orbit.

But then he blinked, his shoulders stiffening coldly. "I must inform you that a painter will be coming on the morrow to commence our portrait as the new duke and duchess."

"So soon?" Clarissa gasped.

"It is tradition," he stated. "And there is no need for us to waste any more time."

Disappointment cascaded over her in waves. Clarissa struggled to control it, to keep him from seeing any of it. And to think that they'd almost had a comfortable moment. The only thing he could think about was his duty.

Clarissa resumed eating her meal, letting silence fall over them. Calum didn't seem eager to continue the conversation and that only ripened her dismay, which then sharpened into determination. She didn't come down here to sit and eat in silence again.

"Have you settled in well?"

His question surprised her so much that her own words died on her tongue. Clarissa blinked at him. He wasn't meeting her gaze, instead plowing through his meal as if he hadn't eaten in days.

"I have," she murmured after a long moment. "Mrs. Dawson and my lady's maid, Sarah, have been treating me rather kindly. And, as odd as it may sound, I think I may have gotten the lay of the manor already. Although…"

"Although?" he probed, raising a thick brow.

Clarissa licked her lips. Now it was her turn to avoid his eyes. "There is one room, in the east wing, that I did not get the chance to see. Mrs. Dawson says that it is off limits."

"You are smart enough to know that I will not answer the question you are about to ask."

His cold tone brought a rueful smile to her lips. "Indeed, you speak the truth, but I am determined enough to attempt it regardless. Is it because of your late wife?"

Calum's jaw ticked, frustration darkening his eyes. Clarissa hesitated, but the question had been plaguing her all day so she couldn't pass up the chance to voice it.

"How did she pass away?"

"Haven't you heard?" he snapped. "I murdered her in a fit of rage."

"I don't believe that."

For some reason, he frowned at her as if he couldn't believe what she was saying.

"It is the truth," she assured him. "I did not believe it for a second. Honestly, I do not know why anyone would think such a thing. I am yet to see this horrible temper they speak of."

"Continue with this conversation and perhaps you will be given the chance."

The words were meant to be threatening. And it was. So maybe that was the reason she let out a small laugh. There was certainly nothing funny about the way he glared at her and yet she couldn't stop herself from giggling.

"Do you think I am a joke?" Calum snarled, his voice cold enough to sober her up a little.

"I do not," she admitted, trying to wipe the smile off her face and failing. "I do not know why I am laughing, honestly. I just think..."

"Think what?"

"That you are pretending to be something you are not."

Clarissa realized a moment too late that she was not making the situation any better. She was prying too deeply into the life of a gentleman who did not want to be seen. And judging by the way he glowered at her, there was only a matter of time before he made her regret it.

That time came so swiftly that she was left gasping in surprise. Calum stood, picking up his glass of wine in a swift motion.

"I have lost my appetite," he announced in a grumble. "I shall be in my study."

He didn't give her the chance to say anything in response. And nothing came to her mind. She could only gape at his retreating figure, realizing that she'd only dug this hole for herself and now he was forcing her to lie in it.

The bang of the door echoed its way into silence. Clarissa sighed to herself. That was nice while it lasted, she thought.

Chapter Thirteen

Waking early was quickly becoming normal for him. At first, Calum told himself that it was because of his nightmares, but there was little intensity to it this morning so he woke calmly, rather than drenched in sweat and heaving.

He told himself instead that it was because his lingering guilt would not allow him to rest. How could he sleep until morning when there were so many things he needed to repent for?

Not for a second did Calum consider the thought that he was hoping to see Clarissa during one of his early morning walks through the manor.

Guilt churned in his gut every time he thought of how he'd ended their dinner so curtly. The moment he'd left the dining room he realized the error of his ways, his anger abating enough to see that perhaps he was overreacting. But he hadn't gone back. Last night, he did what he always did. Locked himself in his study and drank until his mind grew empty.

He wouldn't be surprised if Clarissa was not willing to see him. Surely she'd seen a glimpse of that bespoken anger she'd spoken about. He truly wasn't the kind of man she thought he was. The earlier she knew that, Calum told himself, the better it would be for everyone.

And yet, every time he thought of her, he felt an unusual pang of remorse. Distraction was what he needed, he decided. There were more than enough things on his mind already. He didn't need Clarissa's mood bothering him as well.

The need for distraction brought him back to his study. Rather than heading straight for the sideboard like he usually did, he headed to his desk instead. Stephen had left behind his estate ledgers, urging him to look through them before his meeting with the tenants. A task that loomed in Calum's future like the overbearing sight of dark, stormy clouds.

This morning, however, he picked up the first of the ledgers with ease. He skimmed his gaze over the numbers, mentally calculating the monthly expenses as he went on. He would have to take Clarissa into account now, he realized. She needed pin money and provisions for the future.

Even when he was trying to distract himself, she was still creeping back into his thoughts.

Calum sighed, refocusing his attention on the numbers before him. Stephen was a meticulous man. Everything was written in such fine detail that Calum was tempted to skip over it all.

But then something caught his eye. A discrepancy, numbers that didn't quite add up. Calum frowned, straightening. It was odd for a man like Stephen to make such a mistake.

Calum reached for a plain sheet of paper and his quill pen. Before he could go about figuring out where the error was made, a knock sounded on the door.

"Your Grace?" His butler poked his head in, clearly uncertain. Calum couldn't blame the man. There were a number of mornings in the past when he'd found Calum either passed out on the floor, too inebriated to help himself, or in such a foul mood that it was like walking into the pen of a tiger.

"What is it?" Calum asked, taking measures to calm his tone.

The butler came all the way in. "Mr. Tramp has arrived."

Calum sighed. He'd almost forgotten about the painter. "Is the duchess ready?"

"She is, Your Grace. She is waiting in the parlour for you."

That got him out of his seat. Calum didn't like the thought of sitting still long enough for someone to paint his likeness. But doing so with Clarissa? For some reason, it didn't seem that bad anymore.

As a matter of fact, he quickly left his study and made his way to the parlor. The moment he walked in, his eyes fell on Clarissa. She stood by the small bookshelf, slightly bent to peruse what was tucked within. At his entrance, she turned to him.

A small smile touched her lips. "Good morning, Calum," she greeted.

Calum couldn't find his words. She looked…Indeed, how could one human possess such ethereal qualities? Everything, from the curls in her thick hair to the simple slippers she wore on her feet, was done to perfection. The dress she wore was a deep auburn that made her hazel eyes appear darker than usual and it sat gently on every curve of her body.

"How do I look?"

Calum's eyes snapped to hers. For the first time, he saw

something genuine, something beyond the polite mask she always wore. Nervousness.

Calum cleared his throat, finding it more difficult than it should be. "You look good enough," he muttered.

Despite his lackluster words, her smile brightened. "Wonderful. I wasn't sure about the dress, but it seems we had the same thing in mind."

Calum glanced down at himself, realizing with a start that they were dressed in similar colors.

"You look handsome as well, Calum." She stepped closer. "Calum, I think—"

The door opened before she could get the rest of her words out. His butler entered with Mr. Tramp in tow, a slight man with eyes that darted around the room before coming to rest on them.

"It is good to see you again, Your Grace," Mr. Tramp greeted.

"Let us get this over with," Calum grumbled. The last time he'd seen Mr. Tramp was when he'd met with him to commission a painting with Violet and him. A painting that never came to be. Calum didn't like the wave of bad memories that washed him at the sight of this man.

But as they claimed their seat in the chaise lounge, Mr. Tramp already going about pulling his things from his leather bag, those memories washed away as quickly as they came. The smell of Clarissa's hair perfume came instead. She was close enough for him to feel the heat of her presence yet they did not touch. She smoothed down the front of her skirt, shifting nervously side to side.

"Is it your first time getting your portrait done?" he asked without thinking.

She nodded, biting her bottom lip for a brief moment before she caught herself. "Not since I was a child and I hardly remember it. I am not sure what to do with myself."

"You don't have to do anything. Just sit and wait for him to be finished."

That infernally adorable bottom lip of hers poked out. "Well, that sounds dreadfully dull, doesn't it?"

"I never said that it would be entertaining," he reminded her.

Clarissa speared him with a curious look. "If I didn't know

any better, I would think you were enjoying hearing my complaints."

"Then it is a good thing that you do know better."

She let out a breathy laugh that loosened the knot that had long since formed in the pit of his chest. "Your crassness is more amusing than frightening, Calum. If the latter is your aim then you have failed terribly."

Calum felt his scowl stretch across his face. "I am not attempting to do anything. This is who I am."

"If you say so," she hummed. "How should I pose then, Calum? Should I sit like this?" She straightened her spine and pulled her shoulders back.

"Or this?" She turned her back to him, tilting her head back. Despite himself, his lips twitched, humor whispering through him.

"Or would this be better?" She turned to face the painter again and, without warning, she rested her head on his shoulder. Calum stilled. If she noticed, she made no indication.

His heart began to race. Clarissa had to know what she was doing. There was no way she could not feel the heat emanating from his body or the pounding of his heart like fists against a wooden door. She raised her head and looked up at him with such big, beautiful eyes that every word of protest that rushed to his tongue died.

She was smiling when she looked up at him. But when she met his eyes, it faded. The entire room seemed to disappear entirely. Calum saw nothing but her. The flecks of gold and green in her eyes. The way her lips parted slightly. The gentle tinge of pink spreading across her cheeks.

Mr. Tramp cleared his throat. "May I begin, Your Grace?"

Neither one of them looked at him. The seconds they sat there holding each other's gaze felt like an eternity. But then Clarissa looked away, blinked, and pulled back into herself. He could basically see the mask slipping into place.

"Yes, of course," she answered.

Calum was much slower to recover. It felt like he was poking his head up above the murky waters for the first time in years. When he looked at Mr. Tramp, he couldn't see anything, his mind worlds away.

***

By the time, Mr. Tramp finally called for a break, the painter was thoroughly frustrated. Calum couldn't blame the man, though he felt the same way. Having to deal with someone as uncooperative as Calum throughout the entire process had to be difficult.

Despite it all, Clarissa remained politely patient. But as soon as Mr. Tramp left the room, seeking the refreshments that had been provided for him in the dining room, Clarissa turned to him and asked "Why are you making this so difficult when this was your idea?"

Again, her boldness surprised him. He realized that it had been some time since someone had spoken to him like this. Not even Mrs. Dawson, who had known him since he was a child, dared overstep. Not even Violet, who always knew how to skirt around his moods.

Clarissa seemed hellbent on pulling the truth out of him, no matter how uncomfortable it made either one of them.

"I am not being difficult," Calum protested, hating how childish he sounded. "This is only taking longer than it should. I thought that we would be done by now."

"It may take him a few hours to perfect that scowl of yours."

He frowned at her. And then she blinked. A second went by, then two. Then she burst out laughing.

Calum swallowed thickly. She was utterly beautiful. The polite mask was gone and the true lady underneath had revealed herself. He realized a second later that he loved the sight of her.

"Surely even you can admit that that was funny," she managed in between giggles.

Calum only tried to deepen his scowl but her laughter was infectious. "You seem to be enjoying yourself despite having sat in one spot for hours now."

"I didn't mind at all. I found ways to pass the time. And I was inspired by you."

"Inspired by me?" he echoed dumbly.

She nodded. Her grin was still out with full force. Dare he even assume that she was looking at him with mischief in her eyes?

"I took a sip of the brandy in the corner," she told him,

pointing to the sideboard.

Calum glanced at the sideboard and then back at her, eyes widening. "Are you in your cups, Clarissa?" he asked incredulously.

"Of course not," she said with a laugh. "But I do feel...relaxed. Is this how you always feel? Is this why you chase the bottle every night?"

"You should not play around with such things," he tried to say but she waved him off.

"Heavens, Calum, I am not a child. I am a married woman. The Duchess of Thorneshire. Surely I can have a bit of brandy in what is now my own home. And besides, it helps when having to deal with you. You're...crabby."

Despite himself, Calum let out a short laugh. "Crabby?"

"Yes. Has no one told you that before?"

"I have heard less savory descriptions of my personality."

"Well, crabby fits you perfectly."

"Then what of you? You are nosy and persistent. Perhaps I should have a drink myself to deal with your incessant questions."

"Perhaps you should." She leapt to her feet and made her way over to the sideboard. Calum found himself following after her without thinking. He put his hand over hers the moment she reached for the decanter of brandy.

"You've proven your point," he told her, trying to ignore how close she was. How her breath felt against his skin. "Any more and you will lead Mr. Tramp to believe that you have a penchant for debauchery."

"Is that so bad?" she asked in an innocent tone. "You endure such rumours so perhaps so could I."

"You do not want to be like me."

"You're right. I want to understand you."

Her gaze fell to his lips. And the fragile, fraying string that held his betraying thoughts at bay snapped. He clenched his hands to keep from pulling her into his arms, from pressing his lips against hers to see if they were as soft as they appeared. Clarissa raised her eyes slowly to meet his. There was a challenge in her eyes. Wonder.

Want?

Suddenly there was a knock at the door and, like before, Clarissa was the first to pull away. She did so now with such a bright blush washing her face that he couldn't help but smile.

"Pardon me, Your Grace," said a meek-looking maid as she entered the room bearing a tray of tea and cakes. "Mrs. Dawson asked me to bring this for you."

"Oh, thank you, Sarah," Clarissa rushed to her side. Calum stayed by the sideboard and watched as his wife perused the arrays of cakes on the tray. "My, this looks lovely. Would you like a slice, Sarah?"

Sarah jumped at the question. "I-I couldn't, Your Grace."

"Of course you can," Clarissa plowed on. She sounded a little rushed, as if she was still recovering from whatever just happened between them. "You must have gone through quite a lot in preparing it. Here, have some."

Clarissa offered her one of the slices. Sarah glanced uncertainly at Calum but he said nothing. After a moment, she gingerly accepted the slice.

"Thank you, Your Grace."

"It's nothing," Clarissa said in a tone that implied she truly meant it. This was nothing to her. Kind acts were only second nature.

He was doomed. Marrying her was a bad idea. Being close to her was an even worse one. But now he knew for certain that the life he had lived for five years was about to be disrupted.

And for the first time in years, he felt true fear.

Chapter Fourteen

The day ended slowly with Calum by her side. Even though Mr. Tramp left barely concealing his annoyance at how little painting he'd gotten done due to Calum's constant comments, Clarissa was in a glorious mood.

She'd made him smile. It had been brief, gone as soon as it came, but the effect of it remained. Mr. Tramp left with the promise to return the next day and Calum was quick to leave as well, as if he did not want to be left alone with her.

Clarissa had masked her disappointment with her lingering happiness that she'd made him smile. The mere thought followed her throughout the rest of the day. Even when she had to eat alone in her chambers once more, she felt content. Sleeping hadn't come easy because of Calum. He remained on her mind at every second of the day and when she closed her eyes, he was all she could see. By the end of it, her body had fallen unconscious out of sheer exhaustion.

The next morning came with nothing but excitement. She woke early as usual and, with nothing to do with the enthusiasm thrumming through her veins, she made her way down the drawing room to pass the time. The moment she stepped past the doors, Clarissa drew to a halt.

"Oh, heavens!"

Clarissa watched as the surly duke standing by the window in the drawing room turned to meet her, his arms crossed.

"What is the matter?" he asked in his usual gruff manner.

She could only blink at him, uncertain of what to say. Clarissa knew that he was an early riser but he would spend his mornings in his study. She'd made her way here thinking that she would be alone again.

And to think that she'd been considering spending her morning in her chambers. It was the thunderstorm outdoors that pushed her out of the room after she was finished with breakfast. She'd spent last night curled up in the settee writing her poems, with the storm outside, she thought it would be quite nice doing the same thing with one of the books she'd noticed on the bookshelf yesterday.

"I am just surprised to see you here," she confessed once she had recovered.

"Why?" He faced the window again. "It is my manor."

"That it is," she agreed, drifting closer. She studied the tightness of his stance, his fingers were steepled so tightly that his knuckles were white. As she came closer, Clarissa could see that he was even clenching his jaw.

"What is the matter?" she asked gently.

He said nothing and at first, Clarissa thought that he was going to ignore her. But then he let out a sigh and said, "Mr. Tramp has sent word that, due to the weather, he will not be able to come today."

Clarissa glanced out the window. It was too dark to see anything, the wind chasing away the rainwater that battered the panes. "It would be rather cruel to force him to do so in such a storm as this. Is that what has upset you?"

His jaw ticked. "This will only drag on for longer. I wanted it to be over with."

"Patience, Calum," she said. "Perhaps we could pass the time doing something else."

He looked down at her, brows knitting together. "We?"

"Is that not why you came here? To seek my company?"

His silence said it all. Before he could see her cheeks turning red—goodness, she'd never blushed this much before—she made her way over to the bookshelf. Clarissa pulled out the book of poetry she had been looking at yesterday and brought it to him.

"You were going to read to me that day in the library," she reminded him. "We could do it today?"

Hope tinged her voice. She watched his growing scowl smooth away as he glanced down at the book. Clarissa didn't know if it was the plea in her voice or the title of the book that made his decision. He took it wordlessly and made his way to the settee.

Clarissa took discreet breaths to calm herself as she followed. Alone with him again, she couldn't help but think about what happened during their break yesterday. Their closeness, the tension. The way it felt as if he'd wanted to kiss her. Every time she thought of the ornery duke she had married, she told herself that it was just her imagination.

But was it truly? How could she have imagined the look in his eyes when his gaze fell to her lips? Had it been a trick of the eyes when she saw his head dip towards her for a brief moment?

Whether it was or not, the memory followed her. It was why sleeping had come so difficult to her last night, all but forcing her to retreat to the drawing room to write. Right now it was all she could think about. What it would be like to feel his lips against hers. Should she dare to imagine it?

For a few seconds, neither one of them said anything. Calum only stared at the cover of the book and Clarissa stared at him. She wondered if he was reconsidering his decision. When he shifted slightly, her heart leapt with the fear that he was going to get up and leave her behind again.

Instead, he opened the book. He glanced up at her and her heart skipped a beat for an entirely different reason. For a few seconds, she was frozen in spot as he studied her. She couldn't tell what was going on behind his stormy eyes. But she knew that it was a lot. She knew that his mind raced with the speed of a train like hers did.

Then his gaze landed on something right over her shoulder. Calum frowned slightly. Before she knew what he was doing, he reached towards her. Clarissa sucked in an audible breath when he came close enough to kiss her and she thought that he would.

Like this? her mind screamed.

But no, Calum was reaching for something behind her. Not her. Clarissa felt like she was rushing back to earth when he pulled back with a leather-bound book in his hand.

"I don't recognise this," he said with a frown.

That racing heart of hers fell to the pit of her stomach. Clarissa flew from her spot, trying to snatch it out of his hand despite how unladylike it was of her. But Calum moved quicker than her. He raised it out of her reach just in time.

"Is this yours?" he asked her.

Clarissa avoided his eyes. Her poems were in there. Her precious, sacred poems that have never been read by any other soul. In her exhaustion last night, she must have left it here without realizing it.

"Yes," she pushed out. "It's…private."

Calum's confusion faded into realization. "I see. Is this where you write your poems?"

He still held it out of reach. Clarissa tried not to glance up at it. "I was writing here late last night and I must have forgotten it when I retired to bed."

"I see." Calum gave the book a curious look. "Then perhaps we should read this instead."

"Perhaps *not*," she said quickly.

The strength in her tone must have amused him. That was the only thing she could describe that look on his face as. "Why not? You are a well-spoken lady and have a natural love for poems. I think you must write wonderful ones yourself." He began to unbind the book. "Let us have a look, shall we?"

Clarissa emitted a gasp that, upon reflection, would surely cause her great distress. However, in that moment, her entire concentration was fixed on prying the book from his grasp.

Again, Calum was far quicker than she was. When she launched herself at him, attempting to snatch the book from his hand, he jumped out of the settee. His eyes glittered with certain amusement and surprise but before he could say anything, Clarissa was clamoring after him. She cursed his height when she reached up on her toes and still found herself hopelessly out of reach.

"At this rate, you will begin climbing me," he commented.

"I am not opposed to the idea," she shot back, eyes narrowed on her book. He still held it closed, even though the book was no longer bound. "You won't like what I write. It's all just a culmination of my sordid thoughts written with no order to them. I cannot even call them poems."

"Perhaps I can," he drawled. "Should I take a look?"

He began opening the book. "Calum!" Clarissa shrieked and tried snatching the book again.

This time, he laughed. Perhaps she would have been shocked still at the deep richness of it if she still wasn't so desperate to get her book back. His soft chuckle echoed around them as he stepped out of her reach. They were suddenly locked in a game of cat and mouse. And as the mouse, she was out of her league.

"I shall resort to more violent tactics if you do not hand it back to me," she warned.

Yet again, he did not seem threatened by her. He looked at

her with humor in his eyes, like he found her attempts adorable. "You might hurt yourself, Clarissa."

"And you might—" The rest of her words hitched in her throat when her ankle twisted and the floor was suddenly rushing up to meet her. A strong arm caught her before she fell, but she only threw him off balance. Calum managed to keep a good hold of her as they both crashed back into the settee nearby.

The breath rushed from his lungs, steaming against her hot cheeks. She could feel the rapid pounding of his heart. Or was that hers? The question rushed to the tip of her tongue but stayed there the moment she met his eyes. They searched her own. There was no more amusement, no more curiosity, no more mischief. Just something else she did not know how to decipher, something so strong that it held her captive.

Neither one of them noticed that they were no longer alone until someone cleared their throat. Both their heads turned sharply to the left. Mrs. Dawson stood there bearing a breakfast tray, her eyes light with pleasure and a small smile on her lips.

"Good morning," she greeted.

For half a second, neither one of them moved. But then Clarissa scrambled off his chest, grabbing her book at the same time. She took two large steps away from him though she knew it wouldn't help. Mrs. Dawson had seen enough.

"Good morning," Clarissa managed to greet back.

Calum did not try to recover as quickly as she did. He only straightened in the settee and draped one arm over the back of it as he asked, "How did you know that I was here?"

"I did not," Mrs. Dawson responded as she drew nearer. "I knew that if Her Grace was not in her chambers then she must either be here or at the library. Finding you here as well is only a pleasant surprise."

Pleasant might be too mild a word. Mrs. Dawson looked as if she was trying her hardest to hold back the full force of her smile. She set the tray down on the breakfast table and said, "I shall return with more since I was not prepared for both of you."

Clarissa slid her gaze to Calum, expecting a protest. She thought that he would take this chance to retreat into his shell and state that he would be spending his morning in his study like he usually did. Mrs. Dawson paused expectantly as if she was waiting for the same thing.

But it didn't come. He only nodded. "Very well. Do not be too long. I am starving."

Clarissa didn't have to look at Mrs. Dawson to know that she'd lost her battle on her broad smile. A similar one pulled on Clarissa's lips as well, her chest warming.

"Yes, of course, Your Grace," Mrs. Dawson said quickly before hurrying out of the room.

Clarissa didn't realize that they had been left alone until his steady gaze fell on her once more. She felt a shiver rush up her spine, gooseflesh covering her arms. What would have happened if Mrs. Dawson hadn't walked in when she did?

"Just so you know," he said in a soft tone. "I had no intentions of reading it if you did not want me to."

Clarissa nodded slowly. "I believe you. I just…panicked. I never intended for anyone to read them, you see."

"I understand. But perhaps…" He hesitated.

Clarissa was drawn back to his side without thought. She didn't dare allow herself to get too close, uncertain of what she might do if she did. "Perhaps what?" she urged.

The tentative look on his face only deepened. Clarissa couldn't believe that the usually scowling, crass duke was now avoiding her eyes. "Perhaps one day you could—"

Again they were disrupted by someone clearing their throat. This time, when Clarissa turned to the person at the door, her heart sank at the disapproving glower of Stephen.

"Am I interrupting something?" he asked.

"As a matter of fact, you are," Calum responded before Clarissa could think of a single thing to say. She kept her eyes on Stephen, only because if she dared to turn to her husband he would see how easily he could bring a blush to her cheeks.

"Pardon me then," Stephen responded with very little remorse in his tone. "But there are matters that require your attention, Calum."

Clarissa waited for Calum's protest, certain that he would tell Stephen to leave him be like he usually did. But there came no gruff words of annoyance. Only the shifting of the settee, stating that he was standing without her having to look.

Calum stopped by Clarissa's side. She looked up at him.

Regret was written across his face, so stark that it stole her breath away.

"Another time then," he murmured, as if he only wanted her to hear.

She nodded, her throat thick. "Another time."

And then she was watching him leave again. This time, the pang of loss only followed her excitement for the next time.

***

She didn't see Calum for the rest of the day. When she inquired about him to Mrs. Dawson, the faithful housekeeper only told her that Calum was still busy with his meeting with Stephen. And of course, she didn't know what the meeting was about. Clarissa tried to rein in her curiosity and her disappointment, not allowing herself to go in search of him.

This time when she had her dinner in her bedchamber, she did not mind it half as much. She did so in silence this time, not attempting to cajole Sarah into conversation like she usually did. Clarissa had gotten Sarah to eat with her this time which was progress enough.

Her gaze remained on the dark window, the thunderstorm still going strong. She wondered if it would last another day. If it would delay Mr. Tramp once more and she could spend idle time with Calum.

A sob broke through her reverie. Clarissa looked at Sarah in alarm.

The other girl was desperately trying to hold back her tears and the moment Clarissa's eyes fell on her, she tried to hide her face.

"Sarah?" Clarissa abandoned her meal, turning fully to face her maid. "What is the matter?"

"It's nothing, Your Grace," Sarah pushed out, desperately wiping her tears. They were quickly replaced a second later.

"It is obviously something," Clarissa insisted. "Did something happen?"

Sarah shook her head. She abandoned her meal as well. "No, Your Grace. Please, it's nothing."

"Are you sure?" Clarissa reached out to take her hand. She

didn't want to pry if Sarah was not ready to talk about it but she couldn't help the worry that slipped into her voice.

Sarah's lips thinned. She avoided Clarissa's eyes, staring at her shoes instead. Clarissa waited patiently, pulling her chair closer.

"Your Grace," Sarah finally whispered. "You are far too kind."

Clarissa huffed a laugh. "Is that what has brought you to tears?"

Sarah shook her head, again attempting to wipe her tears. Again, her attempt was in vain. "I just—I can't—" She shot to her feet and sank into a deep bow. "Forgive me, Your Grace."

Clarissa stared at her in utter confusion. Sarah's hands were shaking. As if she just realized it herself, she gripped the sides of her skirt as if she was trying to contain it.

Something else was going on. Clarissa didn't know what it was and she had a feeling she wouldn't get her answer tonight. She quelled her burgeoning curiosity as best as she could.

"You seem tired, Sarah," Clarissa said gently. "I shan't force you to sit with me this evening. I should be the one thanking you for agreeing so graciously even though you must prefer to be someplace else."

Sarah's head shot up, her eyes growing wide with horror. "Certainly not, Your Grace!" she protested. "I enjoy spending time with you!"

Clarissa laughed. "I didn't mean to make you feel bad. And if that is the truth, I appreciate it because I enjoy spending time with you too. But I insist. Go on. You're relieved for the evening."

Sarah's lips wobbled as if she trying to hold back another gush of tears. She bent her head again. "Thank you, Your Grace. Please, excuse me."

Clarissa watched as she left, then let out a breath once she was alone. She hoped another time she would be able to understand what had happened. Because certainly, something had. For now, she hoped that Sarah would not cry herself to sleep.

She turned her attention back to the window, her mind drifting inevitably to her surly husband. Though today she couldn't describe him as such. She'd never seen him look more alive, more human, more beautiful.

A smile touched her lips. She wouldn't hold back tomorrow, she decided. If she wanted to see him, nothing would stand in her way.

Chapter Fifteen

It was odd, Calum thought. He didn't dream that night.

By the time the realization dawned on him, Calum was already getting out of bed. He still woke before dawn, before the rest of the manor was up, and he enjoyed the quiet for a while before the thought struck him.

Violet had not visited him in his dreams last night. He did not dream of her, of death, of his guilt. The last thing he remembered was closing his eyes last night and then nothing.

He didn't know what to do with that knowledge. He'd hated and dreaded the nightmares with every fiber of his being but he'd welcomed it because he deserved it. It was his retribution for what he had allowed to happen. Yet he could not help the whisper of relief that he'd been given a break last night. He'd never felt so rested before, so calm.

That calmness did not last very long. He went to his balcony, that familiar pang of guilt slowly creeping over him as the sky tinged pink with the coming dawn. Calum hardly heard his trembling valet enter the room and throughout the entire process of getting dressed, he'd clung to that guilt. Not at Violet's death this time but at the fact that he had forgotten her, if only for one night.

Distraction, he thought again, when he was dressed. And seeing that Stephen was still pestering him about the tenants, he supposed he could take a look at the ledger books again before setting a meeting with them. Distraction was good. It would help him ignore the tumultuous feelings burrowing into the back of his mind.

The moment he stepped into his study, his gaze fell to his sideboard like he usually did. But he did not feel the usual pull this time. Calum didn't try to question it. He went to his desk and surrounded himself with the stable sight of numbers. They were constant enough to ground him, especially needed since it felt as if he was floating away from everything he had known for the past five years.

A knock on the door pulled him briefly from his ledgers. He was still trying to reconcile the odd mistake Stephen had made when he said, "Come."

He didn't look up when the door opened, focused. But the silence that ensued finally tugged at his attention.

Clarissa stood by the door with a breakfast tray, wearing a nervous smile. "Good morning," she said. "I thought we could have breakfast together."

Calum wondered when the sight of her would no longer feel like a punch to his gut. She looked as fresh as a flower this morning, that thick head of hair of hers piled atop her head like it usually was. Her morning dress, he realized with slight amusement, was the same dark brown as his.

"Come," he said again when he realized she was still waiting for his response.

Her smile widened slightly as she brought the tray over to the settee and center table on the other side of his study. Calum stood, abandoning his task, and made his way over to her.

"Mrs. Dawson told me that you prefer coffee in the mornings instead of tea," she said as she poured him a cup.

"I do." He settled into the armchair across from her. Not because he didn't want to be near her but because he wanted to be far away from her far too much for his liking. "But only because I do not sleep well at night. The coffee helps."

"Did you not sleep well last night either?" she probed.

"Surprisingly, I did not struggle as much as I usually do," he confessed, though he didn't know why it came so easily. "I will still take it since it has become a habit now."

"A man and his habits," she said lightly, sipping her tea. "A bond stronger than no other."

"Are you teasing me, Clarissa?"

"Only paying you back in kind after what you did yesterday," she said easily. He liked that about her. She did not stumble with her words and did not make a show of thinking about what she would say before she said it.

"Fair enough." His cheeks felt odd. A smile was pulling at them, he realized.

"You are yet to read to me, Calum," she pointed out.

Calum studied her as she spread a bit of jam on her toast and took a small bite. Watching her eat stoked his own hunger so he reached for a slice of toast as well. "State the time and place. I prefer to keep my promises."

"Now then?" she asked with a raise of her brow. "The low cadence of your voice while you read will help with my digestion, I think."

"Is that so? And what of my digestion? Should I put it at bay while I honour your request?"

"You keep your promises, do you not?"

Calum chuckled. It came easier to him now, he realized, and he was not in a mood to think too much about why. "You do not allow others to win, do you?"

"I don't know what you mean," she said simply. The humor in her eyes deflated into curiosity. Calum braced himself, already knowing what was going to happen. "Why don't you read anymore?"

He paid keener attention to his meal to avoid her eyes. "There are many things I once took pleasure in that I no longer do."

"Like what?"

"Fencing, for one. I was quite athletic once in my life. Now, I do not know the last time I've done anything physical. I hardly even leave the manor as it is." He laughed humorlessly to himself. He didn't meet her eyes but he felt them burning through him nonetheless. "Eleanor is the only reason I have been in the company of other people in years and she had to force me."

"Is it because of what happened?"

What happened. She was watching her words, making sure not to mention Violet's death too directly. Calum smiled ruefully, wondering just how fragile he must seem if Clarissa was not speaking with her usual candor.

"I'm sure that you can guess," he said after a long moment. "I no longer had a will to live the way that I once had."

"Because of..." She trailed off.

Calum nodded, his throat thick. Suddenly he was there again, with terror pungent in the air and death staining the walls.

Clarissa was quiet for a long while. They ate in silence and the discomfort of his memories began to fade in her grounding presence.

"My father was once a great man," she said at last. Calum's eyes shot to her and she was already staring at him with such intensity that it stole his breath away. "I always thought that way, ever since I was a child. When I was young, he seemed like an immovable mountain that was constant and strong. As I grew older, as I realized his limitations as a human like everyone else, I still saw him as a great man. I had no reason to doubt him, you see. He was a wonderful father, a doting husband, and took care of us."

She poured herself another glass of tea. She sipped gingerly, closed her eyes for a brief moment. "When he died, my impression of him came crashing down around him. I realised that he had been pretending to be something he was not for a long time. I could not help but think that things could have been different if he had just told us. We would not have spent our money with such abandon. We would have been able to talk with him. We would have tried to help leave the gambling dens behind. Sometimes I wonder if the impression we had of him was what forced him into that box. If he felt like he had to remain the perfect father, husband, and baron because that was what everyone else saw him as."

"Why are you telling me this?" Calum asked. He regretted it immediately, realizing that it might sound rude.

But Clarissa's smile was warm as she said, "I did not realise how much I was like my father until he passed away. He would always wear a mask and so did I. I held my tongue and I pretended to be a perfect daughter and perfect lady. I acted as if I was many things that I was not. It led to my father's death and our family's downfall and I vowed that I would never lie to myself or others anymore." She laughed mirthlessly. "I lost a lot of friends. Not only because of the scandal that now surrounded my name but because I no longer held back. They must have realised that they did not like who I truly was."

Clarissa met his eyes. "I have gotten rather good at it, don't you think? Laying it all out for everyone to see?"

Calum was shaking his head before she got the question out fully. "You speak without holding back, I agree. But I can never truly tell what you are thinking."

She raised her brows in surprise. "Is that so? And here I thought that you could tell my every thought."

"If you do then imagine the closed book you would become if you actively attempted to hide your emotions," Calum commented and Clarissa laughed.

"Then if my face does not tell you what I am thinking, allow me to say it plainly. I like the man you truly are, Calum."

His heart skipped a beat. He licked his lips, touched by the warmth in her eyes.

"You were a mask every day," she continued. "I understand why you do, to an extent. And one day I hope to understand more. But I have grown fond of the man behind the mask. And it is my hope that you will not regret locking away who you truly are the way my father did."

Calum didn't know what to say to her. She continued eating as if she understood that and did not expect a response. He could not do the same. He only stared at her, wanting to do so many things at once.

Calum wanted to be closer. To tell her all the things he'd kept in a locked box in his heart. To finally shed that mask she could see through so easily.

He was struck there between decisions, wanting to cling to his past and take a step towards his future.

He was saved by the door opening. Calum realized a moment later that Mrs. Dawson would never enter his study without seeking permission first.

Stephen barely concealed his scowl when he looked at Clarissa. The sight irritated Calum beyond measure.

"It seems I have unknowingly developed the habit of interrupting you two," Stephen commented.

Clarissa turned slightly. "Good morning, Mr. Huntington."

He didn't respond, only gave her a slight nod. Calum's irritation doubled. He struggled to rein it in. He understood Stephen's disposition, understood that his cousin only wanted the best for him. But disturbing his alone time with Clarissa and looking at her with slight annoyance only darkened his mood.

He held it from his voice as he asked, "Is there another matter that requires my attention, Stephen?"

Stephen's lips were in a tight smile. "Not this time, Calum. Other than the pressure I am still receiving from the tenants."

"I said that I would handle it, didn't I? As a matter of fact, I was taking a look at the ledgers to see if my current funds could accommodate any request that they may have. There is something that seemed odd to me."

Calum stood and made his way to the desk. He held up the already-opened ledger for Stephen to see.

Stephen took the book from Calum with a frown. His eyes skimmed the pages, landing on the error after a few seconds. There were a few moments of silence as he studied it. He pushed his spectacles up his nose. "It seems as if I made a mistake," he said at last.

"It would appear so," Calum agreed. "You do not usually make mistakes."

"I must have been tired when I made his entry. Human error. I shall fix it."

Calum nodded, making his way back to his seat. He was more than happy to leave that in Stephen's hands. "I figured as much. I tried attempting to do so myself but it meant I would have to go back several years, which would take far more time. Since you are more accustomed to the bookkeeping, you will fare better at it than I will."

Stephen frowned at him. He hadn't moved from the desk, only turned to face him. "You were going to fix the error yourself?" he asked incredulously.

It was Clarissa who spoke next, her voice tinged with confusion, "Is that so difficult to believe?"

The question made Calum chuckle. "I have left much of my estate affairs to Stephen. I know almost nothing about what has happened regarding the bookkeeping in five years."

"There is no need for her to be privy to such details," Stephen said tightly.

"Why not?" Calum asked. "She is my wife, after all."

The statement surprised them all. Stephen gave him a horrified frown that took a few seconds too long to tuck away. And Clarissa blinked rapidly at him before a broad smile stretched across her face. Calum chose to focus on the latter.

Clarissa recovered after a few seconds, though her adorably pink cheeks still betrayed her pleasure. "Would you like to join us, Mr. Huntington?"

"I do not," he answered coldly. "I only came here to inform Calum of something."

"Go ahead," Calum urged, reaching for his coffee again though it was no longer as hot as he'd like.

Stephen hesitated, glancing balefully at Clarissa.

"Very well, then," Calum spoke again. "Then let us discuss how to approach the tenants. After you fix the bookkeeping error, of course. I cannot do anything without the proper numbers."

"There is no need," Stephen said, a little too quickly. "I only came to inform you that you have received your annual invitation to the upcoming village spring fair."

"Spring fair?" Clarissa echoed excitedly.

"Does that interest you?" Calum asked her.

She nodded, eyes glittering. "I have never attended one before but it sounds intriguing. When will it be?"

Calum looked expectantly at Stephen and his cousin pushed through tight lips, "It will be in two days. But I intend to inform the village head that you will not be attending as usual—"

"Accept the invitation," Calum said without thinking. His attention was on Clarissa, her palpable enthusiasm infectious. "If it is you would like to go," he added, his tone a little uncertain.

"I would love nothing more," she assured him with a bright smile.

Calum felt a shade of that smile touch his lips as he looked at Stephen. "Accept the invitation," he said again.

Stephen was quiet for a long moment. Then he said, "As you wish. Please, excuse me."

He turned and left as quickly as he came. Calum barely watched his retreat.

"You will undoubtedly turn a few heads if you go," Clarissa pointed out after a moment.

Calum shook his head. For some reason, the thought didn't feel like a noose tightening around his throat like it once had. "They will be too busy staring at you to pay me any attention."

"Wondering what lady would be mad enough to marry the monstrous duke?" she asked in a teasing voice.

"Wondering what a lady with your beauty sees in a man like me," he responded seriously.

Her smile slipped. She swallowed. "They won't think that," she murmured.

"I beg to differ."

The pink of her cheeks gave him far too much satisfaction. Calum silently vowed to spend as much time as he could coaxing it out of her time and time again.

He ignored the nagging thought in the back of his head that told him that this was a bad idea. He was getting too comfortable with Clarissa. He was forgetting something very important. Someone very important. He was too happy, too quick to smile, too quick to laugh. This was not him.

Calum tucked all those thoughts away, along with the mask he'd finally allowed himself to shed.

Chapter Sixteen

The next two days passed quickly and slowly at the same time. Clarissa was happier than she'd felt in days. Calum was more attentive than he'd ever been before. They ate breakfast, lunch, and dinner together now, talking about everything and nothing all at once. Though they never touched on the topic of either one of their pasts—and she did not voice her question about the tenants, not wanting to break the fragile atmosphere surrounding them—Clarissa felt as if she was getting to know the true duke a little better.

When the time came for her to get ready for the spring fair, she was a bundle of excitement. Clarissa said as much to him during breakfast in the morning and he laughed—a sound that always lifted her spirits—telling her that she was like a child being told they could go to the confectionery shop.

Clarissa agreed. She hadn't felt excited for something like this in such a long time. Dregs of it had swarmed her when she'd prepared to attend Lady Yulebridge's ball but it had been overshadowed by her apprehension at the fact that she had to make an impression. At that time, too many things hinged on performing well at the ball rather than having fun. But now that she had none of those worries, she was eager to simply enjoy herself.

And enjoy herself with Calum. She still couldn't believe that he had agreed to go, even though it was just a few short hours from happening. The man who hated being in the presence of other people had not hesitated to state his intentions of attending all because of her. That touched her in ways she could not express.

"Your Grace?"

Sarah's voice pulled Clarissa from her thoughts. Clarissa closed her book, one she had been staring at but hadn't been reading for the past hour now. "Is it time to get ready for the fair?" she asked breathlessly.

Sarah blinked, taken aback by the urgency in Clarissa's voice. "Yes, Your Grace. And these came for you as well."

Sarah held up four letters. She brought them over to Clarissa who only frowned. One from Louisa, another from Martha, and another from Nora. It was her mother's letter that surprised her the most.

Clarissa opened Louisa's first. It was long, a barrage of questions and exclamations of how much she missed Clarissa and wished that she could visit. She peppered Clarissa with questions about Calum, asking her if she was all right or if she had fallen victim to the duke's temper. By the end of the letter, Louisa seemed to be desperately trying to hold in her hysteria, as if every word she'd written only increased her worry.

Martha's was much calmer. She asked how she fared her time with the duke as well but she did not speak with any judgment. Clarissa recalled how certain her aunt had been about Calum's innocence. It shone in her letter, telling Clarissa how much they all missed her and that she hoped she was happy.

Nora's letter was also long—though not as long as Louisa's—and it was endless questions. Disbelief turned to curiosity to acceptance. In the very last paragraph she expressed how happy she was that Clarissa was married and that, while the rumors inspired worry, she hoped that Clarissa was content with her decision. The sentiment touched Clarissa. Despite Nora's nosiness, there was no hiding that she truly did want the best for her.

Her mother's was nothing but two sentences.

Tell me that you are all right. I worry for you.

Tears pricked Clarissa's eyes. She could imagine her mother's lifeless form lurching into action long enough to scribble these few words before going back to staring at nothing. The last she'd seen them, they'd been convinced that Clarissa was going to live with a madman. And she hadn't made any attempt to assure them that she was fine.

She blinked the tears away and left the letters on the end table nearby. "Sarah, please remind me to write back to them in the morning," she said thickly, even though she doubted she would forget.

"Yes, Your Grace. Shall I pick out your dress?"

Clarissa just nodded and Sarah got into action. She moved to Clarissa's closet and began sorting through the appropriate dresses to wear to a nighttime event. Clarissa studied her and after a long moment, she said, "You seem to be in better spirits."

Sarah jolted at the observation. She avoided Clarissa's eyes.

"I feel better, Your Grace."

"That's good to know. Will you tell me what happened?"

"It was nothing, Your Grace. I only felt a little overemotional."

That wasn't the full truth but Clarissa nodded nonetheless. "It happens to the best of them. Next time, you don't need to hide your tears from me."

Sarah was shocked enough by that statement that she forgot she was trying not to look at Clarissa. "I couldn't possibly do that!"

"Why not?" Clarissa asked as if it should be obvious. "Unless I make you uncomfortable?"

"I..."

"I understand that our titles may separate us in your mind but it does not in mine. I hope you will feel comfortable with me to speak freely." Clarissa paused for a moment, then laughed. "I'm suddenly realising how nosy that makes me sound."

Sarah swallowed, pulling free a soft green dress. "Will this suffice for this evening, Your Grace?"

"It is lovely," Clarissa agreed. She knew she couldn't pry anymore, even though she wanted to. She did not want Sarah to feel any more uncomfortable.

But Sarah's brows remained slightly pinched throughout the entire process of getting her ready. They did so in silence, which Clarissa did not mind since it was clear that Sarah was lost in thought. Whatever it was weighing on her mind was considerably heavy, Clarissa thought.

After a while, she was finally ready for the spring fair. Clarissa had asked Sarah to style her hair simply, wanting to feel relaxed. She didn't think it would be anything like the stuffiness of a London ball, after all.

Clarissa left Sarah behind in the bedchamber and made her way down to the drawing room to wait for Calum. She didn't make it there. She came to a halt at the top of the staircase when she spotted him pacing back and forth in the foyer.

She rarely got the chance to admire him for long. What was usually seconds before he noticed stretched on for nearly a minute as she watched him walk back and forth, clearly troubled by something. At first, she'd only stopped to admire him, impressed yet again at the fact that he was wearing a deep green waistcoat.

At this point, surely he was inquiring about what she would wear before she did.

But then his deep frown was what drew her attention instead. He must be thinking rather deeply about something if he did not notice that she was there. Clarissa slowly descended, her hand running down the balustrade.

"Calum?" she called when she came to the last step and he still hadn't noticed her.

He looked startled, whirling to meet her. His frown smoothed away. "Clarissa," he breathed. "You look..."

Clarissa felt a flush of heat as his eyes trailed down the length of her and then back to her face. "Great minds think alike," she commented, gesturing to his waistcoat.

Calum glanced down at himself and chuckled. "Others might think that it was planned."

"Which makes it even nicer that it wasn't." She came closer, heart racing. "How are you feeling?"

The question softened his eyes. "A little apprehensive," he admitted, to her surprise. "But since it will be under the cover of night, perhaps no one will pay me much mind."

Without thinking, Clarissa slipped her arm through his. He was warm to the touch. "I am willing to believe that they will not even notice that you are there."

Calum chuckled. "Is that supposed to make me feel better?"

"Am I doing a good job?" she asked hopefully.

"You are, though you've opted to take an interesting approach."

This time, Clarissa laughed. "Then that is all that matters. Now let's go. A night of fun awaits us."

***

The nearby village, only a twenty-minute ride away from Thorneshire Manor in the opposite direction of London, had come alive. Clarissa didn't know the state of the village when they were not engaged in a fair but if it was anything like this, she would come here every day.

As darkness blanketed them from above, lanterns were strung from every tree interspersed throughout the village square.

There was a large well sitting in the very centre of the square and everyone convened around it. Vendors selling sweet treats and hot, easy snacks. Men and women playing an array of stringed instruments and flutes. The tune they created was lively and exciting enough to inspire nearby dancers. Clarissa stared openly and enviously, wishing that she knew the steps to the dance.

She didn't know where to look first. So many things were happening at once and it seemed like everyone in the village had decided to attend. She was so wrapped up in trying to take it all in that she didn't notice that others were staring at them.

Calum seemed uncomfortable. He must have noticed the stares as soon as he arrived. It was one thing to be a tall, handsome duke but another thing to have such a horrible reputation attached to your name. He quickly became the subject of nearby whispers, some openly staring while others gave him discreet glances.

Clarissa slid her arm through his, pulling his attention away from the lingering stares. "Where should we go first?" she asked him.

"I don't know," he answered. "I have not been here in years. Much has changed and yet everything feels the same at the same time."

His gaze trailed away, landing on a group of men who didn't bother to hide their curiosity at his presence. Clarissa could all but feel the discomfort spreading through him. "Then do you know the steps to that dance?" she asked, indicating to the couples skipping around to the beat of the music.

Calum shook his head. "Long ago I did. If I attempt to do so now, I will only make a fool of myself." His shoulders sagged. "I'm sorry."

"There's no need to apologise," she told him with a smile. "We can go and see the stalls instead."

Calum nodded, only barely masking his reluctance. This was incredibly uncomfortable for him but Clarissa was sure he would relax soon enough. It was normal for people to be surprised at his sudden appearance. But after a while, no one would pay him any mind.

She desperately hoped that her assumptions were true.

For now, she was content to simply stroll along, taking in the sights. There were so many things to see. They came upon a stall of confectionery, surrounded by children begging their mothers to purchase something for them. Calum offered to buy some sweets for her but Clarissa shook her head, claiming she wanted to save her appetite for whatever else the fair had to offer.

They moved on to another and another and another. The stares followed them as they went but Clarissa didn't miss the fact that they grew less intense. Just as she'd suspected, the shock over his presence was beginning to wear off. Calum must have noticed it too because he was beginning to relax.

"I won't take no for an answer," he said suddenly.

Clarissa raised her brow at him. "Pardon me?"

"You have said no to everything I have offered to purchase for you since arriving." They came to a stop at a stall selling flowers. "But this time I will not allow you to deny it."

Clarissa's cheeks began to hurt from the force of her grin. "I shan't stand in your way then. But be warned: I am quite picky when it concerns gifts."

"I think I will be able to manage," Calum said confidently which made her laugh.

The vendor's eyes widened when Calum approached. Those who had already been standing at the stall stepped out of his way, not bothering to hide their stares. Clarissa stood slightly behind him and offered them kind smiles, to which they returned tentatively.

"A bouquet of lilies, please," Calum said. "And that." He pointed to something Clarissa didn't see.

"Yes, of course, Your Grace." The vendor hurriedly put his bouquet together as well as whatever he had pointed to. Calum caught the eye of one of the men staring at him and gave him a brief curt nod. The man was surprised to return it and Calum was already stepping away.

"How did I do?" he asked her. If he was aware of the fact that others were still staring, he didn't make any indication.

Clarissa observed the bouquet with crippling happiness. She'd never thought about what her favorite flowers were. She liked them with the same simplicity as anyone else who liked pretty things. But right now, lilies were her favorite. "You did perfectly," she murmured.

"Then this should have your heart swelling with happiness," he said, his tone a little smug as he reached up and tucked something into her hair. Clarissa touched it, feeling around the soft petals. He studied her face with a soft smile. "You look..."

Clarissa raised her brow at him. Now she didn't really care that they were still the center of attention by the stalls. "Beautiful? Stunning? Gorgeous?"

He let out a breath. "Ethereal. Sometimes I wonder if you are human."

The words were said with such seriousness that her smile fell away. "I am human, Calum. As human as you are."

He swallowed, his eyes filling with the words he didn't seem to know how to say aloud. Clarissa took his arm again, her bouquet tucked in the other. They continued to the other stall and she wondered if he'd forgotten about everyone else like she did.

Eventually, they came up to a puppet show that was already well underway. Calum was about to move along but she held fast, entranced by the show. It was mostly being watched by the children of the village but there were a number of adults around the edge of the onlookers, laughing at a joke she did not understand just yet.

"Do you like things like this?" he asked, his nose wrinkled slightly in distaste.

Clarissa smiled up at him. "How can you not?" she countered.

Calum blinked at her, then turned his attention back to the puppet show like he was seeing it through new eyes. "Perhaps it is not so bad," he said after a long while and Clarissa considered that a win.

Eventually, her eyes trailed away from the entertaining performance to the laughing children. The oldest among them seemed no more than ten years. Clarissa wondered what it would be like to have one of her own, to see her face reflected back to her in her spawn. She'd never thought much about it before, beyond just an inevitable event that would happen in her future. But now, with Calum by her side, the idea lingered in her mind.

She sneaked a glance at him. Despite his earlier words, he seemed engrossed in the performance. At one point, his frown of concentration cracked with a chuckle.

Our children will be beautiful.

She hadn't realized that she'd spoken aloud until he looked at her in alarm. "What did you say?"

Clarissa quickly looked away. "Nothing," she mumbled.

"You said that our children will be beautiful. Is that what you have been thinking about?"

She avoided his eyes, staring at the puppeteers though she hardly focused on them. "It was just a passing thought. Nothing to pay any interest to."

Clarissa felt his eyes boring into the side of her face. She tried to ignore it as best as she could, bracing herself for his response.

At last, he looked away and Clarissa let out a silent breath of relief. Soon enough the performance came to an end and the puppeteers took a break. Clarissa and Calum silently made their way to the next attraction but her mind lingered with the dispersing children. The terms of their marriage had been looming over them this entire time and Clarissa had been content to ignore it if Calum was.

Now she couldn't help but wonder how long she would be forced to pretend that it was not there.

Chapter Seventeen

Calum wasn't given the chance to lament the fact that he and Clarissa were the subject of attention. No longer. Not when he quickly found himself immersed in everything the fair had to offer.

It had been so long since he'd last attended one. He didn't focus on the memory of the last time, in the early days of his courtship with Violet. He'd brought her to one of the fairs only shortly after meeting her and had been convinced that night that he was in love. The memory crept over him as they walked, as Clarissa clung to his arm and *exclaimed* at everything she saw. He expected frustration, anger, pain.

Instead, he felt content. He felt happy. So engrossed in the present as he was now, he did not feel the sharp stab of the past.

A tremor of guilt rushed through him at the realization but Calum quickly dismissed it. This evening was not one to focus on bad emotions. Even if he wanted to, Clarissa would quickly nip it in the bud, whether she did it on purpose or not.

Her excitement was contagious. She marveled at everything she saw, forgoing the option of sweet treats for smoked meat and different kinds of bread instead. Calum admired the way she devoured everything with all the grace of a queen. She was too perfect, he thought again. And she was not even aware of it.

Clarissa clung to her bouquet of lilies the entire time. Now and again, she would reach up and brush her fingers over the flower he'd tucked into her hair and a small smile would touch her lips. That alone made attending the fair—despite the bad memories it dragged up—completely worth it.

Clarissa slowed her pace. Her attention was on yet another stall, selling decorative pins, combs, and colorful ribbons. Calum watched as she brushed her fingers over an ornate comb.

"Do you want it?" he asked.

She looked startled at his question, which confused him. He'd quickly offered her anything she'd glanced at for more than a second all evening. Right now, Calum would purchase everything being sold at the fair if she stated that was what she wanted.

He tried not to think about the implications of that fact. He only focused on her, like he had been doing all evening.

"It's lovely, isn't it?" she asked, picking up the comb. "I think Louisa would really like it."

"Louisa." Calum had to think for a moment. "Your sister."

"Yes, my sister," she confirmed with a laugh. "She enjoys things like these. I wonder if I should get this for her for when I visit."

"Which will be?"

Clarissa shook her head. "I do not know yet. But I think that it must be soon. I miss them."

The wistful note in her voice was like pins through his heart. He hadn't even given her family a second thought. But Mrs. Dawson had said it, hadn't she? Clarissa was lonely. All this time he thought that it was because she was in an unfamiliar place with no one to speak to but perhaps it was because she was just homesick.

"How about you pay them a visit on the morrow?" he suggested, surprised at how difficult it was to get the words out. He didn't want her to leave so soon, he realized, even if it would be for a short while. He'd only just gotten used to her presence.

Clarissa smiled at him as if she knew exactly what he was thinking, even though Calum had made sure to wipe any reluctance from his face and voice. "I will think about it. But for now…" She turned her attention back to the array of combs.

She picked up the one she had been looking at and continued her perusal. As she went on, she ducked under a few ribbons dangling from the top of the stall. A blue one got caught in her hair but she went on without noticing it.

Calum approached the vendor. It was an elderly woman with black hair tucked under a colorful scarf. She watched him with steady green eyes. "Anything she touches is hers," Calum informed the woman, his eyes still on Clarissa as she trailed along the side of the stall. "As well as the ribbon now stuck in her hair."

The woman nodded. "As you wish, Your Grace."

Calum's eyes followed Clarissa. She picked up another comb, a brush, and a set of decorative pins before returning to his side with a bright smile. Without meaning to, his answering grin pulled at his lips.

"For Louisa," she said, holding up the comb. "For Martha." She showed him the decorative pins. "And this brush is for my mother. I hope they like them."

"I'm sure that they will." Calum glanced at the vendor long enough to tell her to charge him before returning his attention to Clarissa. His gaze was constantly drawn to her, he realized. Like a moth to a flame, he could not keep her out of his sight.

"And this," he added, pulling on the ribbon that was still stuck in Clarissa's hair. "May I?"

Her eyes widened in surprise, then softened. Wordlessly, she nodded. She turned and tilted her head slightly away, allowing him to wrap the ribbon around the full head of hair, tying it in a neat bow at the nape of her neck.

Clarissa faced him again, eyes fluttering shyly. "How do I look?" she asked him yet again.

And yet again, Calum could only find one proper description. "Like an angel."

The tinge of her blush was an expected and welcomed sight that warmed him from within.

"Your Grace."

It took a moment for him to realize that the vendor had spoken again. He looked at her. "What is it?"

She placed all of Clarissa's items in a tiny drawstring bag without looking, her gaze boring into him. "Would you like to have your fortune told?"

The denial was on the tip of Calum's tongue but before he could get it out, Clarissa jumped in. "I would absolutely love that," she gushed happily.

The vendor nodded as if she'd expected nothing less. She wordlessly handed the bag of Clarissa's items to Calum then gestured to Clarissa to follow her.

She was a gypsy, Calum noticed a bit later. If her dark hair and colorful clothing hadn't given it away then the garishly painted caravan she led them to, did. He felt a thread of discomfort when the woman looked at him again, as if she was seeing something she should not be. But Clarissa's excitement stilled his tongue.

Getting one's fortune told was a silly thing to do, Calum believed, but he was willing to endure the silly things for this one night. Even so, when the woman raised an expectant brow at him, he shook his head. "Only for her," he told her.

"If you wish, Your Grace," the woman stated and almost sounded a little weary.

Clarissa was thrumming with enthusiasm. She sat daintily on the small stool in front of the caravan while the woman pulled up another in front of her. Calum didn't know what he was expecting. Perhaps a crystal ball or something to that effect. But the woman only took both of Clarissa's hands in hers, closing her eyes.

Silence fell over them. It was an odd sort of quiet that blanketed the small space by the caravan despite the revelries still happening around them. Calum felt a shiver race down his spine as he watched the woman. He could see her eyes moving behind her closed eyelids, her fingers gripping Clarissa's hands too tightly for his comfort.

Seconds stretched on and his discomfort grew. Just when he was about to stop what was happening, the woman's eyes flew open, a silent gasp on her lips.

"What is it?" Clarissa asked breathlessly. "What did you see?"

The woman released Clarissa's hands and shook her head sadly. "You are in danger, Your Grace."

Calum's heart sank.

"Danger?" Clarissa repeated. "What do you mean?"

The woman just shook her head, looking between Clarissa and Calum with undisguised pity. "Your past, present, and future is intertwined with mortal peril. You are in grave danger, Your Grace. You must leave—"

"Enough!" Calum's bark was enough to draw the attention of those nearby. He didn't care. He caught Clarissa's wrist, pulling her behind him. "You speak nothing but nonsense."

"I have seen the future, Your Grace," the woman said, sounding dismayed. "And it ends in nothing but certain destruction."

"I said, *enough*!" This time his shout was loud enough to command the attention of that entire section of the fair. The woman only continued staring at him, this time with pity.

Clarissa put a gentle hand on his arm. "Calum—"

"We're leaving," he stated, turning sharply on his heels. He pulled Clarissa along behind him. "I knew that that was a foolish idea from the start. I should not have patronised such idiocy."

"Calum," Clarissa called from behind him but he didn't answer her. His throat was thick with anger, his vision blurred from the force of it. Without warning, Violet's still body lying in bed flashed in his mind's eye. He gritted his teeth.

"Calum, you're hurting me."

That brought him to a halt. They'd almost made it to the carriage now, mostly out of earshot. He looked down to realize that he had been gripping Clarissa's wrist so tightly that his knuckles were white. He let go immediately and she tucked her wrist to her chest.

He knew there was a question in her eyes. Calum couldn't allow her to voice it. He didn't look at her, stalking towards the carriage in brisk strides.

Clarissa quietly followed. His rage thrummed through his body with such overpowering force that he did not even have the strength to offer her any explanation for why he was being like this. How could he when all he could think about was the gypsy's words?

Mortal peril.

Danger.

Destruction.

Those were all words that had been associated with Calum after Violet's death, running rampant throughout England and painting him as a monster. He'd allowed those words to truly become who he was because he thought he deserved it. And just when he'd lowered his guard, they were coming back to haunt him.

He helped Clarissa into the carriage and climbed in after her. The moment the carriage set off, he turned his attention out the window, avoiding Clarissa's pressing eyes. She said nothing and he didn't know if that was a good or bad thing.

For now, the silence was the only constant he could drown himself in. He needed it to fish out his discarded mask and secure it back in place.

He could have sworn that Clarissa sighed.

Chapter Eighteen

Calum retreated to his chambers the moment they returned to the manor, pushing out a clipped '*goodnight*' before leaving her behind. Clarissa didn't take her eyes off him until he was out of sight. Only then did she release the heavy sigh that had been building in her chest on the way home and made her way to her room.

That night, she could barely sleep. She was plagued by the brief look of horror that had seeped into Calum's face moments before he'd exploded in anger. It was gone almost as quickly as it came but Clarissa could not get it out of her head. Her wrist still throbbed from the way he'd gripped it but she welcomed the pain. It was nothing compared to what he had to be enduring.

The next morning, she rushed through getting dressed, hurrying down to the breakfast parlor in the hopes that Calum might be there. And he was. The moment she spotted him, Clarissa felt a dizzying wave of relief. She'd been afraid that he'd resorted to locking himself away in his study again. And who knew what self-damaging habits he might have fallen into?

Calum noticed her a bit later and he straightened. A brief, uncertain smile flitted over his lips. "Good morning, Clarissa."

"Good morning, Calum," Clarissa returned, trying to keep the relief from her voice. She crossed over the room to him. "How are you feeling?"

If she didn't know any better, she would think he looked a little sheepish at the question. "Better. I must apologise for—"

"There's no need," she quickly said. "I understand."

He didn't need to explain what he had already made so obvious. What the fortune teller had said had pulled on memories he was yet to heal from. Memories that had kept him locked away in his manor like the beast they said he was. He'd only just decided to take a step away from that man and look where it brought him.

One day, she hoped that he would be comfortable enough to talk about his late wife. Clarissa knew that there was far more lurking under the surface. She'd gotten a peek at it last night.

"Besides," she added in a chipper tone. "I do not take the theatrics of the fortune teller seriously. If she had told me that I was destined to live happily for the rest of my life, it would be rather dull, don't you think?"

Calum frowned at her, clearly not knowing whether or not to laugh. "One would think that they would be happy to receive such a fortune."

"But that is not what will gain her any popularity, I'm sure." There was already tea and toast laid out. Clarissa reached for the teapot to pour herself a cup. She looked out the window, eyes falling on the gentle stretch of grass just beyond.

"You're wearing the ribbon," Calum commented, sounding slightly awed.

Clarissa touched her hair, smiling. Despite her rush this morning, she'd asked Sarah to tie the ribbon in the back of her head. "It has quickly become my favourite accessory," Clarissa confessed.

"Something as simple as that? I can buy you far more beautiful accessories if you say the word."

"I shan't, though I appreciate the sentiment. As simple as it may be, I was touched when you got it for me. I think I shall wear it every day, even if it does not match my dress."

Calum chuckled at that and Clarissa could tell that he was pleased by what she was saying. Her chest felt warm, her stomach like a million flowers were unfurling within.

"How is your wrist?" Calum asked. His tone was darker, more serious. She glanced up at him to see that his attention was on her hand—and the slightly purple bruise tinging her skin.

She resisted the urge to hide it from his sight. "It hurts," she admitted, only because she doubted he would believe her if she lied. "But not bad. Please, don't worry about it."

"How can I not when I am the one who did it to you?" His voice was thick. His throat bobbed. Clarissa could see his restraint on his emotions—anger or otherwise—threatening to snap. "I should not have—I cannot—"

"You did not mean it, Calum," Clarissa said gently. "And it is fine. Please, believe me. Would I lie to you?"

"You would if you thought that you had a reason to," he answered without hesitation.

Clarissa couldn't help but laugh at that. "Fair enough. But please believe me when I say that I am quite all right."

He wasn't convinced. That much was clear. His attention remained on her wrist, staring at it with a frown of concentration. Clarissa could only imagine the self-deprecating thoughts rushing through his mind. She wished she could soothe him in some way. She wished she could take him in her arms and tell him that there was nothing he needed to worry about.

She couldn't deny that she felt a spark of fear at the fortune teller's words at first. But that had quickly dissolved as reality set back in. She was safe here. Calum would not hurt her, no matter how much others might think the opposite. No matter how much he might be beginning to believe the same thing.

"Did you enjoy the fair?" she asked, hoping to turn his attention to better topics. "Other than the last bit, of course."

He blinked, as if her question brought him out of a trance. "Surprisingly, I did."

"Why surprisingly? Did you not think that you would?"

"Not at first. I have avoided the spring fair for more reasons than wanting to remain out of the public eye." He hesitated then poured himself some coffee as if he needed something to do with his hands. "There are too many memories surrounding my last time."

"What sort of memories?" she asked softly.

Calum swallowed thickly. He didn't speak for a while. Clarissa was about to say that he didn't have to tell her anything if he did not want to talk about it, but then he said, "The last time I went, it was with my late wife."

Her heart thudded against her chest. This was the first time he'd ever mentioned her himself. "And you did not enjoy yourself at the time?" she asked, speaking lightly even though the atmosphere had quickly grown serious.

Calum huffed a humorless laugh. "I did. I always did. Growing up, I would attend the spring fair every year, and that year, I took her with me. It was when I first realised that I was in love with her."

A sudden pang hit her chest at the admission. Calum was not meeting her eyes. His attention was on his food and he ate as if it were life and death, as if daring to allow himself to stop would only bring on waves of memories he would much rather suppress. Clarissa stared at him, studying the almost always present knit of brows that only smoothed away when he laughed or smiled. She watched his jaw move and tick as he ate, his large hand wrapping around his cup. She studied the flop of his dark hair and the unending stretch of emotions in his gray eyes.

It hit her so forcefully that she lost her breath. She loved him. Without realizing it, she had fallen hopelessly in love with him.

Hearing him speak about his love for his late wife, even though that was what she'd wanted, was more difficult because of it. Jealousy whispered through her, quickly followed by her shame. She should not feel such things she knew. But to think that Calum had once been able to show such love so freely, to know that the man he once was may never reappear felt like daggers to her chest.

Suddenly, Clarissa no longer wanted to hear. She hated herself for her selfishness. Who knew when he would be comfortable enough to speak about this again? It would be good for him to say these things aloud after spending five years keeping them locked away. She knew that even as she bit on her tongue and focused on sipping her tea.

She felt his eyes on her but she refused to meet them. She hoped that he wouldn't ask, hoped that he would not continue. At least not for now.

"Enough of my sordid past," he said at last. "There is something I have been wanting to ask you."

"What is that?" she asked, still not looking at him.

"Would you be interested in having a picnic with me tomorrow?"

The question brought a surprised gasp from her lip. Calum blinked at her, then chuckled.

"Is my invitation so outrageous to have elicited such a reaction?" he asked.

"Yes," she answered without hesitation. A smile she could not hold back even if she tried, stretched across her face. "I would love to."

"Good." He looked relieved. Surely he hadn't thought that she would say no? "Do you have plans for the rest of the day?"

Clarissa's heart began to race. "I haven't given what I shall do today much thought."

"Then we should resume the portrait sittings. Mr. Tramp has agreed to remain on call for us."

Clarissa tilted her head to the side. "Here I thought you were going to offer to spend some time with me."

Calum met her gaze. He seemed to be holding back a smile. "Haven't you grown bored of my presence yet? I thought you said I was crabby."

"I am growing to like your crabbiness," she confessed.

He must have lost his battle because the smile came out with full force. The sight threw her, sent her heart careening against her chest. Calum reached behind him, stretching for a book that she hadn't noticed sitting on a nearby end table. He held it up with a quirking brow.

Clarissa nodded, smiling in return. She settled back, sipping her tea as Calum opened the book and began to read. She didn't recognize the poems but it didn't matter. Listening to the soft baritone of his voice, the rise and fall of it, and catching his eyes every time he glanced up at her only chased away the lingering feeling of envy that had taken root in her heart.

She didn't care about his past, didn't care about who he'd loved before. In this moment—this utterly beautiful moment—all she cared about was him.

A resounding crash sent her hurtling back to reality. Clarissa gasped but Calum was already on his feet, making his way to the door. "Stay where you are," he ordered sharply.

Fear clogged her throat. She watched as he approached the door, peering outside with his features taut. For a moment, the fortune teller's words came rushing back to her. *You are in danger*.

But then Calum released a long breath of frustration. He raked his hand through his hair, turning back to face her. "It is nothing," he told her.

"I fail to believe that," she protested, already on her feet. Her heart still fluttered as she made her way to his side.

Shards of what was once a vase littered the floor. "Someone must have knocked it over when they were passing by," Calum explained, sounding incredibly irritated.

"And simply left it there?" Clarissa asked. It was not a long hallway. If someone had knocked it over, they would have gotten the chance to escape before Calum made it to the door.

"Perhaps they did not want to get in trouble. I have a fearsome reputation, after all."

That made sense, Clarissa conceded. But as she stared at the broken vase, she couldn't help the trepidation rising through her. She kept it from her face when Calum took her hand.

"Come," he said. "I shall ring for Mrs. Dawson and she'll clean it up. I don't want you to get hurt."

That was enough to assuage the anxious feeling wrapping her in its embrace. Clarissa nodded and allowed him to lead her over to the settee this time. Then, after ringing for Mrs. Dawson, Calum fetched the book and came to her side. He sat closer than he usually did, as if he knew that she was still frazzled by the broken vase.

Clarissa listened to him read from the book of poems, ignoring the fortune teller's ominous prophecy echoing in the back of her mind.

Chapter Nineteen

Calum's hand itched with the urge to reach out and take Clarissa's. She was walking so close to him. Once or twice, her hand brushed his as if in invitation. As if she too wished to curl her fingers around his.

Perhaps he was a coward, Calum thought. Or perhaps he was simply too shy—a description he never once thought he would apply to himself—but he did not make the move during the entire trek through the forest.

Calum had told her that they had to travel through the forest for a short while before making it to the meadow. Before the apology for such an uncomfortable trip could leave his lips, Clarissa had perked up at the mention of the forest. "Let's go then, shall we?" she'd said, her voice tinged with excitement. "No need to waste time here."

Calum had grinned and swallowed the words on the tip of his tongue. The path through the forest was well-traveled, wide enough that it didn't feel as if the thick birch trees were encroaching on them. Sunlight filtered through the canopy ahead and birds flitted in and out of the cover of leaves, filling the air with their song.

As they walked, they talked about simple things. Mundane topics that Calum once hadn't had the patience for. It was a wonder he had the mental capacity to engage in conversation with her when all he could think about was how nice it would be if they could make their trip to the meadow hand in hand. A sappy, sentimental thought, and yet it plagued him so thoroughly that he took to glancing at her the entire time.

The moment they delved out from the forest and onto the small circle of land filled with swaying grass and wildflowers, Calum glanced at her once more. She looked lovely and he was pleased to see that she'd worn her ribbon like she'd promised. She caught his eye and he couldn't find the strength to look away. Clarissa smiled.

"You look ravenous," she commented.

Calum nodded. He knew what she meant and yet couldn't help but say, "I am." *In ways that I thought had long gone dormant.*

"Then have we arrived? I'd hate for your growling stomach to disrupt the singing of the birds."

Calum chuckled. He caught her hand, not allowing himself to deliberate on it any longer. He caught a glimpse of her smile as he tugged her along.

They went to the center of the meadow before Calum set down the picnic basket Mrs. Dawson had prepared for them this morning. He laid out the blanket first and couldn't help staring at her as she settled upon one side of it, tucking her legs to the side of her. She pulled her hair over one shoulder then caught his eye with an expectant raise of her brow.

"What's the matter?" she asked.

"Nothing," Calum said quickly. Because how would he begin to explain the tumultuous feelings that raged within him at watching that simple act?

She didn't probe him, though her gaze did not lift. Calum felt it watching her every move as he took out the arrays of cakes, sandwiches, and teas that Mrs. Dawson had packed.

Clarissa laughed. "She must have gotten a little overexcited."

"God, that woman," Calum grumbled with no annoyance in his voice. "You should have seen her face when she handed the basket to me. You would think that I was heading off to be knighted by the Prince Regent."

"She must be relieved that you are making attempts to spend time outdoors after five years spent locked away in the manor."

"Undoubtedly," Calum agreed. "Though I think she is happier at the fact that I am not doing so alone"

"As am I," Clarissa said softly. When he looked at her, she quickly looked away. "You seem close to her. Mrs. Dawson, I mean."

"She was like a mother to me," Calum explained. He went about arranging all the food before turning to face Clarissa. She reached for a small sandwich. "Despite the fact that I was the duke's son, she did not treat me as if I was royalty. She would often scold me like I was her own."

"How unusual," Clarissa murmured and he nodded.

"Unusual, yes. I think I might have been drawn to her because of that. She treated me like I was human. Of course, as I grew older, she began showing me the respect that was to be given to the heir of the dukedom but only when we were before company. Alone, she went back to being that warm, motherly figure I always loved."

"What of your own mother?" Clarissa asked. "The late duchess."

"My mother was kind and gentle and supporting in her own way. But she was a duchess, and before then, the daughter of a duchess. Being raised by a lady who placed such weight on societal duties had its limitations. I remember being passed between my governess and the maids. Mother would come to see me now and again but I did not receive much of her attention until I was old enough to sit with them during dinner."

Clarissa levied him with a pitying look, which made him laugh. "She was a good mother," Calum told her. "I do not think I am making that clear. Only in a different manner, that's all."

"I understand," she said. As usual, he believed her when she said that. He didn't doubt for a second that Clarissa empathized with him, even if she'd never been through it herself.

"And what of you?" Calum asked. "Were you close with your mother?"

"Once upon a time, I was," she confessed. "When I was beginning to grow into my womanhood, we grew closer, becoming something more akin to friends than mother and daughter. But that was before my father died and we lost everything. That was before her mind snapped."

Calum imagined Lady Quelshire sitting at the table during their first dinner together. He remembered how she'd stared listlessly at the table, not having a single bite of food. She looked like a shell who only knew how to breathe.

Clarissa must have seen the look on his face because the tilt of her lips lacked its usual delight. "I believe that the weight of everything that occurred was too much for her to handle. When my uncle took us in, it took a lot of convincing to get her to leave our home. And for two years she would only sit at the window in the drawing room and stare."

"That must have been hard on you."

"It was hard on all of us. It felt as if I lost both parents at once. All of a sudden, the burden of our family was on my shoulders."

"Is that why…"

"Why I agreed to marry you so readily?" she asked before he could force the rest of his words out. He swallowed, unsure of whether he wanted to hear the response. "It was. I was desperate, though I tried my hardest not to seem that way."

"I did not think that you were," Calum assured her. "You wished to be married, like nearly every other lady in London, yes. But desperate? Not at all."

Clarissa laughed. "That's good, at least. When I first met you at your aunt's ball, I was trying my hardest not to show it."

"And I was trying my hardest to ignore how nice it felt to dance with you."

The words were out before Calum could stop them. Clarissa's brows shot to her hairline and he tried not to avoid her gaze.

"I thought you hated me," she told him.

"I wanted to hate you, just like I hated everyone else in the ballroom. It bothered me that I did not."

"You had looked so troubled then."

"And I do not look troubled now?" he tried to tease.

But she didn't laugh. "You do not, though I know that there is so much more healing left for you to do."

Calum could only stare at her. He didn't know why he felt the urge to speak, to reveal things he had long kept hidden in his heart. He tried biting on his tongue, wanting to keep this fragile part of himself closed up in his heart.

But Clarissa trapped him in the steadiness of her stare and all but pulled the words to the tip of his tongue.

"Do you know how my wife died?"

Chapter Twenty

Clarissa swallowed, trying not to react too strongly to the question. "It was due to natural causes," she told him.

Calum barked a laugh so bitter that it surprised both of them. "You might be the only lady in England who believes that."

"Is that not what happened?"

"It was. Yet somehow, everyone believed that I had succumbed to my anger and brought her to her demise. I loved her with all my heart and everyone knew it. Yet they were so quick to dishonour our love with such malicious rumours."

His pain was palpable, waves of it thickening the air around him. He clenched his jaw so tightly that Clarissa was a little afraid that he might break his teeth. She wanted to go closer, to take his hand. But she was frozen to the spot as she watched him delve into the past. She could all but see him reliving that terrible time all over again. The pain, the fear, the horror that raced across his features in quick succession tore her to shreds.

"What happened?" she asked softly.

Calum's eyes snapped to hers, smoldering. "She died on the night of our wedding. No warning, with no harm to her. Just death."

Clarissa didn't hold back this time. She crept over to his side, taking his hand in hers. He stared at their entwined fingers as he fell back into the past.

"It happened over the course of one long painful hour that felt like an eternity," he explained softly. "Nothing was amiss before it. One moment she'd retreated to her bedchamber to change out of her dress while I waited for her in the parlour. The next, I heard screams. When I arrived, I think I knew that she was already gone but I refused to believe it. I called our physician and after spending a painstakingly long time in her room, he only confirmed my worst fears."

"It was not your fault," Clarissa said softly because she knew that he blamed himself. She was aware that he secluded himself as a result of his sorrow and the remorse that plagued him deeply.

Calum clung so desperately to her fingers that they began to hurt. "I should have been there to stop it. I should have done something. I should have known."

"You could not have known," Clarissa insisted. The pain etched into his face was so heartrending that she could not stop herself from throwing her arms around him. She didn't want him to see the tears she shed for him so she waited until he would not hear it in her voice. "It was not your fault, Calum."

"They believe that I killed her," he rasped. He was not successful at hiding his tears like she was. "At first it angered me that they would think that. I may have had a bit of a reputation as a hotspur before but how could they think that I would ever lay a hand on her?"

"They are foolish," Clarissa soothed. She began to stroke his hair, consoling him like she would a child. He sank into her embrace. "They know nothing."

"I allowed myself to believe it after a while. I might not have murdered her with my own hands but she died under my watch. She was my wife and I failed to protect her."

She swallowed past the lump in her throat. Hot tears blazed separate paths down her cheeks but when she began to shake, she realized it was due in part to Calum. He sobbed in the crook of her shoulder, tears already soaking through her dress and chemise to touch her skin. He made no sound and yet the force of his weeping made them both tremble.

Clarissa pulled away, framing his face in her hands. She'd never seen him like this before, so utterly broken. His nose was already red, tears running unhindered one after the other. She wondered if he had given himself to properly mourn or if he had simply locked himself away like a martyr. How many years of tears worth was this?

"I did not know her but if she loved you the way that I do, she would not want to see you like this." Calum's eyes widened slightly at her confession but Clarissa went on, needing to get it all out. Needing him to understand. "She would not want to see you become shades of who you once were, blaming yourself for something that you had no hand in. Five years, Calum. You spent five years punishing yourself for what happened. Do you not think that it is time to forgive yourself? How many years of your life will you spend in such pain?"

Clarissa didn't know what came over her. His sadness pulled

on something deep within her, making her act without thinking. She wanted—no, *needed*—to show how tender and beautiful love could be, that he could one day open up his heart again and that she would be here for him when that time came.

She kissed one eye, then the other. Gently, she wiped his tears and was a little pleased to see that no more came to replace them. Calum seemed too stunned to cry.

"What did you say, Clarissa?" he whispered.

Heat touched her cheeks though she did not look away from his eyes. "I said many things. If I repeat myself, I doubt I will be able to do so in the exact same manner."

Her attempt at lightening the mood only fell flat. His hand reached up to touch her cheeks and he straightened. Clarissa realized suddenly that she had sunken into his lap.

"You said you love me," he murmured.

She tried her best not to look away even though she knew what was to come. He was in no space to return her feelings. She only hoped that he would make an attempt to dull the sharp sting of rejection.

"I do," she said softly. "And I will—"

She didn't get the chance to finish because his lips were on hers. They were soft at first, tentative. He was waiting, she realized, for her to push him away.

But she leaned into him instead, inviting him in. She had dreamt about this moment for so long these past few days but nothing could compare to the actual moment. The tenderness of his lips, the collision of their hearts against their chests, the way their bodies fused together as if this moment had been destined.

This was what the fortune teller should have informed her of. Perhaps then she would have been a little more prepared.

All too soon, the kiss came to an end. Even as Calum pulled away, he kept close to her, their breaths intermingling. They were both breathing heavily as if they had just run for miles. Calum pressed his forehead against hers and she closed her eyes. She wanted this moment to last forever.

Then, a soft rumble broke through the suspended moment. They both froze and then Clarissa giggled.

"I think we should get some food in you," she said softly.

"Not yet," Calum protested. His hands fell to her waist and

he hadn't pulled his forehead from hers.

Clarissa was more than content to wait for as long as he wanted to. But then his stomach growled again, louder this time, and he laughed instead.

"All right, it seems it will not rest until it is fed," he sighed.

Clarissa was tempted to mimic his sigh as she crawled out of his lap. Alone like they were, she didn't care about how unladylike her position had been. Besides, they were already married. There were so many things they could do now that such limitations were not placed on them.

Calum caught her hand as she pulled away, keeping her from going too far. She grinned broadly as she settled by his side. Without saying a word, he reached for a sandwich, his eyes finding hers again.

She didn't care to explore the reason why he didn't say the words back to her. She didn't care. The kiss, the way he kept her by his side, the comfortable silence that had settled over them.

It was far better than what those two words could ever provide.

Chapter Twenty-One

It had been some time since Calum had last been here. Weeks, he realized. From the moment Clarissa came to be his wife, he had not thought to come back.

Now, remnants of his previous guilt speared him as he stared at the wooden door. The hallway was as dark as it had been since that time. Despite the fact that he'd forbidden anyone from entering the room, Mrs. Dawson had made sure to keep the corridor spotless. Where there should have been layers of dust to greet him he saw nothing but shining surfaces and shadows lurking in every corner.

It hurt to be here. It hurt that he had not come here in some time. It felt like he was forgetting her and that was enough to let that guilt blossom in his chest.

But he had come here to finally confront his past. He knew that it wasn't going to be easy but he hadn't expected this breed of fear.

With a slightly trembling hand, he reached for the door handle.

The room was the exact same way he'd left it. Small but every surface of the floor was crammed. Trunks with a heavy layer of dust were stacked in the four corners of the room. An easel and an unfinished painting caught his eye and he was suddenly pulled into the memory of Violet sitting in the sunroom of her old home, commencing her watercolor painting. On the day of their wedding, she'd had all her painting supplies brought to Thorneshire Manor. She never got the chance to finish it.

Everything else she owned was tucked away in one of the trunks. Calum was hit once again by the mark she had left behind. She'd possessed so much and everything that had once been hers carried a piece of her. It was why he'd locked them away. When he wanted to be surrounded by her presence, he came here to immerse himself. To cry. To grieve.

Today he felt...acceptance.

Calum closed the door behind him, his eyes falling on the portrait Violet had also brought from her old home. She was a few years younger in the portrait than she'd been when she died.

Calum remembered how excited she had been to put pieces of herself throughout the manor, to make her mark here as she did everywhere else she went. It was why she'd wasted no time in having her things packed and sent over. He recalled how she'd laughed when she said that she would hang this portrait in the main drawing room for all their guests to see.

"*They will think that I lived here all my life,*" she'd say.

Calum's heart felt oddly still. He didn't move from the center of the room, drinking everything in. After his picnic with Clarissa yesterday, after her confession, Calum knew that things could not remain the same. The man who clung to the past with such a fierce grip could not see a future with her. And he wanted a future. It surprised him just how desperately he did.

But he couldn't love her the way that she deserved if he did not let Violet go.

Something caught his eye. A flash of blue in a room of dusty white and brown. Calum frowned.

It was a slip of fabric on the floor underneath the unfinished painting. Calum's chest grew cold when he realized what it actually was. A ribbon.

He stalked forward, snatching it from the floor. There was no denying it. It was the same ribbon he'd bought for Clarissa. She'd come here knowing that he'd forbidden it? After he'd bared his heart and soul to her yesterday, how could she have betrayed his trust like this?

Rage, hot and familiar, filled him at once. He clenched his fingers over the ribbon and marched out of the room, slamming the door behind him. He hardly saw the path before him. Calum knew exactly where to go, his legs taking him there before his mind had the chance to catch up. His fury was an emotion he understood. It overrode his earlier acceptance like a raging river washing away any remnants of a drought.

He banged open the door of the library. Clarissa, who had been seated within, jumped in fright.

"Calum?" Her eyes went wide at the sight of him. She began to rise but when she saw the fury on his face, she froze. "What happened? What's wrong?"

The concern in her voice only spurred his anger. How could she look at him like that? He wanted to believe that this was just a mistake but the truth of what happened was clenched in his fist. He would not allow her look of horrified innocence to be his undoing.

"You betrayed me!" he hissed.

As he advanced on her, Clarissa quickly got to her feet. As if she wanted to meet his rage standing, despite the confusion clouding her hazel eyes. "What are you talking about?"

"Did I not say that no one was to enter that room in the east wing?" He was shouting. It had been some time since he'd roared like this. Calum didn't like the sound of it. A voice in the back of his mind told him to calm down, to speak rationally. He didn't need to talk at the top of his voice to show that he was upset.

But the flash of hurt across her face dug so deep that he wasn't sure how well he'd be able to follow his own advice. "I didn't go there," she tried to say but he stalked away from her before she could get her words out. "Calum, you must believe me. I will admit that I was curious but I would never—"

"Don't lie to me," he snarled. He held up the ribbon. "I found this inside the room. Why else would it be there if it hadn't been you?"

Clarissa stared at it as if she couldn't understand what she was looking at. "I don't know how that got there. I admit that I found it odd when it was missing this morning but—"

"Enough with the lies!" He grabbed the first thing he could get his hands on. Yet another vase fell victim to his rage as he flung it across the room. It shattered to pieces just seconds before Stephen stepped into the room.

His cousin observed the wreckage before resting his eyes on Calum. "If you insist on throwing a tantrum, Calum, perhaps you should close the door first."

Calum grumbled a curse, raking his hand through his hair. The servants were bound to think he'd gone back to his tempestuous ways.

But when he looked back at Clarissa, that was the least of his worries.

Her eyes shone with tears, her bottom lip trembling from the force of it. Both her hands were clenched into tight fists at her side as if she was using every fiber of her strength to keep from breaking in front of him. As swiftly as the rage had come, his guilt came chasing after it.

He let out a breath of frustration. "Clarissa—"

"I do not understand why my ribbon was found in your room." Clarissa's voice was soft. It was that gentleness—gentleness that he did not deserve—that deflated the rest of his anger. Despite it, she spoke firmly. "But I will not apologise for something that I did not do. The fact that you will not even allow me to speak the truth as I know it before throwing your assumptions around and giving in to your anger speaks to the respect you have for me."

This situation, this horrible situation he'd created, was spiraling out of control. Calum hated to see the hurt in her eyes even though he met it. Even though he deserved it. Panic seized him.

"Forgive me," he tried to say. "I do not know what came over me. I—"

"You did not give me the chance to offer any explanations or defense so I will not allow you one."

She started forward. Calum felt a knot form in his throat as she brushed past him. He reached out to grab her wrist, to stop her, to apologize. But he was frozen. Not by the accusation in her voice but by the tears she could no longer keep at bay.

Calum didn't watch her leave. But he listened to her footsteps for as long as he could before he let out a long, deflating breath.

"I have just made a mess of things, haven't I?" he spoke aloud.

Stephen approached him from behind. "Surely you do not believe what she is saying, do you?"

"She says that she did not do it."

"You found her possession there. If she did not do it, who did?"

With Clarissa's last words hanging over him, Calum couldn't care less about that anymore.

Chapter Twenty-Two

Clarissa didn't know how she made it to her bedchamber. Her knees buckled as she hurried past the threshold and it took too much of her strength to pull herself to a stand, to trudge over to her bed before throwing herself against the pillows.

Sobs racked her body with such force that it seemed to shake the bed. She didn't bother to hold back her wails. It was muffled into the softness of her pillows, echoing around her ears. There was so much pain, too much hurt for her to deal with right now. She couldn't. She couldn't do anything but cry.

She didn't know when someone else came in. She only felt a hand on her shoulder after what felt like forever and Mrs. Dawson's gentle voice saying, "Your Grace."

Clarissa didn't stop to think. She sat up and buried her faced against Mrs. Dawson's bosom, bawling. Without hesitation, Mrs. Dawson wrapped her arms around her, stroking her back gently.

"It's all right, child," Mrs. Dawson murmured in soothing tones. "Everything will be all right."

"He's horrible," Clarissa sobbed. "How could he think that I would do something like that? How could he—he—" She couldn't get the words out anymore. They seemed to burn her throat as if they were blasphemy.

"He does not know what he says," Mrs. Dawson was saying. She stroked Clarissa's hair like her mother once did when she was a child. It made her cry harder.

"He's utterly foolish for even thinking it!" Clarissa cried.

Despite it, Mrs. Dawson's chest rumbled with her laugh. "That I cannot deny. Cry, my dear. It will make you feel better. Sarah?"

"Y-yes, Mrs. Dawson?" Clarissa hadn't known that Sarah was here as well. Her lady's maid spoke in a startled tone as if she wasn't expecting Mrs. Dawson to address her.

"Go and fetch Her Grace some tea."

"Yes, Mrs. Dawson."

Clarissa listened to Sarah's retreat with half an ear. Her crying still hadn't abated. She hadn't bawled like this since her father died. At that time, she'd done so in fits and bursts, only ever when she was alone. She'd had to remain the pillar of strength for her family so she hadn't allowed herself to shed any more than the proper tears that were expected of a daughter mourning the death of her father.

This was nothing like that time. It felt as if her heart was twisting in her chest, stripping off in tiny little pieces to only lengthen her pain. Mrs. Dawson patiently held her as she cried and cried. Until her throat grew hoarse and exhaustion hung heavily upon her.

At long last, Clarissa pulled away slightly to show that she was done crying. She felt numb. She didn't know how much time had passed. Mrs. Dawson kept her hands on her shoulders as if she was afraid that Clarissa would collapse if she didn't. She felt so tired that she couldn't blame the housekeeper for her precautions.

"Lie down, Your Grace," Mrs. Dawson suggested gently. It was 'Your Grace' again. Not 'child' or 'dear'. She was the duchess and Mrs. Dawson was the housekeeper. Mistress and servant. Clarissa mourned Mrs. Dawson's gentle tone but when she looked up at the older woman, her warm smile settled her a little bit.

"I have never seen His Grace like this," Mrs. Dawson said. She still stroked Clarissa's hair. Clarissa stared up at the ceiling, glad that she'd at least expended her tears.

"I thought he was known for his temper," Clarissa murmured hoarsely. "I am the one who should have expected to be at the receiving end of it eventually."

"No, not like *that*," Mrs. Dawson pressed gently. "His Grace has always been quick to anger ever since he was a child. I will admit there was once a time he'd learned how to quell his temper but the past five years had undone much of that progress. But then you arrived."

Clarissa sniffled. When she closed her eyes, she saw his look of betrayal behind her eyelids. When she opened them, she saw his rage-filled glare embedded into the ceiling. She couldn't escape. "I have done nothing to change him."

"I disagree. He is not the man he once was. Dare I say that he has become a better man than I have ever seen him, even if he has not shown it just now."

Another tear crept down the side of her face even though she thought she was done with them. Clarissa threw her arm over her face. "That does not make me feel any better, Mrs. Dawson," Clarissa confessed. "I understand what you are trying to do, but Calum's actions speak volumes."

"That much is certain," Mrs. Dawson agreed. "I will not tell you to forgive him. I am in no place to say such a thing to you, Your Grace. My only hope is for you to understand that you have helped put together a broken man. And it is my hope that you will not give up on him."

And with that, the tears came rushing back. Mrs. Dawson stayed by her side, stroking her hair as she waited for it to pass. Sarah had slipped back into the room without Clarissa realizing it. Or perhaps she just could not hear anything over her own sobs.

"Your tea is here, Your Grace," Mrs. Dawson said. "I shall leave it at your bedside. Please do not let it get cold. I shall...go to check on His Grace."

Clarissa did not want her to leave but a selfless part of her knew that Calum might need Mrs. Dawson's presence more than she did. So she said nothing, listening to Mrs. Dawson's retreat. After a moment, she felt another weight against the bed. Sarah was still here.

"Your Grace," she said softly, her voice cracking as if she too were on the verge of tears.

"I am a pitiful sight, aren't I, Sarah?" Clarissa managed to say.

"Of course not, Your Grace."

A wobbly smile tugged at Clarissa's lips and was gone a second later. She sat up, her face heavy from the force of her crying. She knew her eyes were already getting swollen.

If she didn't think she looked quite the sight, the expression on Sarah's face confirmed it. Clarissa tried to smile to assuage her lady's maid's worry. "The tea, please."

Sarah's lips thinned. She didn't move right away. Then with trembling hands, she picked up the teacup and saucer. She held it out to Clarissa but before she could take it, Sarah pulled back. "The tea has grown cold, Your Grace. I should get you another."

"I only need something to wet my tongue," Clarissa assured her. "Cold tea will not bother me."

Sarah still looked uncertain but she handed over the teacup nonetheless. Clarissa felt her worried gaze on her as she took one sip, then two. Before she knew it, she was finishing the entire thing. Clarissa set it down herself.

"How do you feel?" Sarah asked timidly.

"Calmer," Clarissa said. "And so tired. Forgive me but I wish to be alone."

"Yes, Your Grace." Still, Sarah seemed hesitant to leave.

Clarissa huffed a laugh that sounded breathless and flat, undoubtedly inspiring more worry in her maid. "I promise you that I will be fine."

Sarah nodded, though her lips remained thin with disbelief. She crept out of the room, not taking her eyes off Clarissa until the door finally closed.

Alone, Clarissa curled onto her side. The smile she'd forced onto her face fell away. She couldn't bring herself to think about anything else but the way Calum had shouted at her, his words like daggers slicing through her fragile sensibilities.

They had warned her, hadn't they? He may not have put his hands on her but his words had felt like he'd struck her all the same. A part of her understood his frustration. Such a sacred part of his past had been wrongfully encroached upon. Deep down, she knew he had every right to be upset.

But to be upset at her? To deny her a chance to explain herself? To truly believe that she was capable of doing something like that to him?

That was her undoing. Clarissa didn't know when it would stop hurting. It felt as if her chest was caving in on itself and her heart was splitting into a dozen pieces in order to avoid being crushed.

I should give him a piece of my mind.

The thought invigorated her. Clarissa sat up, forgetting the burdensome exhaustion that had held her captive just moments ago. She wouldn't let him force her into solitude while she inevitably cried herself to sleep. She would tell him just how much he'd angered her, sharpening her tongue against him as he had done her.

Clarissa stalked down the hallway, knowing exactly where she would find him. If she was right, he would surely have locked himself away in his study again. She wondered if he had taken back up drinking again and tried to ignore the pang of concern at the thought.

Just as she whirled onto the corridor where his study was, a wave of dizziness sent her careening against the wall. Clarissa gasped. Her vision began to blur, the corridor stretching endlessly beyond. She tried to straighten but her legs failed her. Without meaning to, she fell to the floor.

Mrs. Dawson appeared before her. One moment she was exiting Calum's study, the next she was running down the corridor toward her. Clarissa thought she might have seen panic on the older woman's face.

"Your Grace!" Mrs. Dawson screamed. Or at least, she suspected that she might have screamed. Sounds were nothing but a dull buzz in her ear but Mrs. Dawson's voice cut straight through to her core. Clarissa held a hand out to her, a murmur of help on her lips.

Clarissa didn't get the chance to see if Mrs. Dawson ever made it to her side. The darkness claimed her before then.

Chapter Twenty-Three

He didn't know what to believe. His truth or Clarissa's?

His truth now sat on the desk in front of him, taunting him. That lovely blue ribbon now brought a bad taste to his mouth, the memory attached to it soured by betrayal.

But was it truly betrayal? Clarissa told him that she didn't do it. Would she have lied to his face like that?

It went against everything he knew about her, everything he wanted to believe. A shadow of shame turned his insides to ice when he realized how quickly he'd jumped to his conclusion. He hadn't even given her a chance to explain herself before he'd assaulted her with his accusations.

"I see you contemplating the matter, Calum," Stephen's calm voice broke in. "And it will do you no good."

Calum slid his glare to his cousin, who stood in the corner of the study with his arms folded. "Why did you follow me here?"

Stephen seemed unperturbed by Calum's obviously lingering anger. "I wanted to make sure that you did not do something foolish."

"Like what?" Calum spat. "Empty my sideboard?"

"It would not be the first time."

Stephen was right about that and that only served to irritate Calum further. He stalked away from his desk to the window. Maybe if he turned his back at everything, this confounding situation would sort itself out.

"It was her, Calum." This time, Stephen's voice was softer. Gentle. "I know you do not want to believe it. I can see that you two have grown close as of late. But now her true colors have been revealed. She has no qualms with encroaching on what you deem to be private and she has the gall to lie to your face—"

"Do not speak of her that way!" Calum barked. He turned his head in time to see Stephen stiffen in the corner.

His cousin was quiet for a long moment and then he said, his voice laced with frustration, "How shall I speak of her then, Calum? Shall I sing her praises when it is clear that she has shown that she is a wolf in disguise?"

Calum whirled on him. The fury that had abated just mere

seconds ago went flaring up in him again. "You have no right to say any of this! You do not know her!"

"Neither do you!" Stephen did not shout. He didn't need to. But his voice echoed with the same fierceness as Calum's. "If you did, you would not have doubted her in the first place."

"I—" He broke off, words failing him. Stephen was right. Calum hated to admit it, so he kept his mouth closed and stalked back to the window. But there was no denying the obvious truth. He'd doubted her because a part of him truly believed that she might have done it.

Tension seeped into the silence between them. Calum's mind drifted back to the tears he'd seen glimmering in Clarissa's eyes. He could still almost hear the hurt in her voice. His heart twisted in his chest.

"Your Grace?" Mrs. Dawson's voice sounded at the other end of the door, followed by a knock. "May I?"

Calum contemplated sending her away. Before he could decide fully, she entered. He could feel her gaze burning into the back of his neck.

"Forgive me for interrupting, Your Grace," she said. "But I have come to inform you that Her Grace is now resting in her chambers."

Calum thinned his lips. He turned, meeting Mrs. Dawson's eyes. Pity shone back at him.

"How is she?" he managed to push past his suddenly tight throat.

"She is...distraught. But calm now."

Distraught. He could see her now, crying into her pillow, cursing the day she'd met him. Shame and guilt gutted his insides.

"Does she...do you think..."

He didn't know how to get the right words out but it seemed Mrs. Dawson understood. "I think you should give her some time before you go to visit her, Your Grace," she said. "I do not think she will take kindly to your company right now."

"I understand." But hearing those words only tore at him. Now he wanted nothing more than to march to her bedchamber and beg for her forgiveness. He was willing to forget about the ribbon. To forget about the fact that someone had entered the room he'd forbidden all from going near. If it meant that she might forgive him, he was willing to forgive himself for how disgracefully he'd acted.

Mrs. Dawson must have sensed his internal struggle because she said, softly, "I'm sure she will understand, Your Grace."

Calum nodded, throat bobbing. "I hope so."

There was a flash of pity in her eyes before she began to retreat. Calum turned to the window.

"Your Grace!"

Mrs. Dawson's scream of horror sent his heart sinking. The world seemed to slow down as he whirled back to face her, just barely glimpsing the petrified look on her face at something in the hallway before she darted away. Calum raced out the study behind her.

He'd never seen Mrs. Dawson run the way she did now. For a brief moment, he was confused and it mingled unpleasantly with his trepidation. But then she sank to the floor of the corridor over a heap of brown tresses and long skirts and that feeling gave way to pure, unadulterated terror.

He was by her side in a second. Calum wasn't aware of moving, only that one moment he was watching his housekeeper sinking to the side of his wife's lifeless body and the next he was scooping Clarissa into his arms with two words echoing in his mind.

Not again not again not again not again

Panic crawled up his throat. He was moving again, his instinct telling him to bring her back to her bedchamber. Calum didn't dare look at her face at first, afraid of what he might see. Afraid that he might notice something similar to what had happened five years ago. But when he made it to her room and laid her on her bed, he couldn't hold back any longer.

Her face was as pale as the sheets she laid on, her forehead dotted with sweat. She was breathing, thank God, but it was shallow and quick and so soft that he had to put his ear to her lips.

"What happened?" Calum felt like he'd been pulled out of his body, hardly aware that he had spoken aloud until Mrs. Dawson's panic-filled voice spoke back.

"I don't know, Your Grace," she said hurriedly. "She was fine when I left her chambers."

"Call Dr. Marsh," he rasped. He didn't take his eyes off her, didn't allow himself to look away for a second. "*Now.*"

"Yes, Your Grace." Mrs. Dawson was out the door a second later.

Calum felt as if everything in him had stopped. He hardly knew how he was breathing. With trembling hands, he reached out to take Clarissa's. It was hot to the touch. Her face was still, her lips parted slightly as if her body knew that she would not survive breathing through her nose.

That night five years ago came rushing up to choke him. He didn't feel the tears on his cheeks. Gently, he reached out to touch her cheek, dread swallowing him whole at how hot she was.

"Please," he murmured. That was all he could manage. A small prayer to her, to God, to anyone who might be listening.

He couldn't go through this again. Especially when he hadn't even gotten the chance to tell her that he loved her too.

***

Dr. Percival Marsh had always been a sprightly man but it seemed he had aged significantly in the five years that Calum had not seen him. Calum only briefly took note of the way he walked, as if he could no longer stand up straight, when he hurried into the room and threw down his leather bag. Gray laced his hair, his green eyes cloudier than they'd once been.

"Your Grace." Dr. Marsh's eyes darted to him for only a moment before focusing on Clarissa. She'd only gotten worse in the time it took the physician to arrive. Calum had taken to keeping his fingers on her pulse to ensure that she did not slip away from him.

"Save her, doctor," Calum pushed out. He couldn't manage anything more than that. The fear that had settled into his bones was enough to keep him subdued. He could only focus on taking one breath after another. If he dared do anything else, he might find himself sunken in the same dark hole of despair he'd only just managed to crawl out of.

All because of the lady now laying prone in bed.

"I need the room," Dr. Marsh said at last. His voice sounded thick with an emotion Calum could not name but then the physician was moving, getting into action.

Calum didn't want to leave. The last time he'd done that,

he'd only closed the door on the truth of what was to happen—that he was going to lose the best thing in his life. Calum wasn't sure he could survive such pain twice.

But he did as he was told, silently. He hesitated at the door, another prayer on his lips, "Please."

He didn't give Dr. Marsh a chance before he closed the door.

Mrs. Dawson and Clarissa's lady maid were on the other end, both wearing identical looks of abject worry. Thankfully, they both had the good sense not to say anything. Calum's nerves were frayed to the point of snapping and he didn't have a clue how he might react if they'd dared speak.

Instead, he simply turned and made his way down the corridor. Mrs. Dawson fell in step behind him. Silence followed them all the way to his study. Thankfully, it was empty. Calum didn't know where Stephen might have gone and he didn't care right now.

"I'm sorry, Your Grace," Mrs. Dawson murmured. She had the good sense to keep the door open. Calum had no intention of staying here for long. He wanted to be close to Clarissa, but standing around in the hallway would only distress him further.

So he stalked to the sideboard, the familiarity of his actions calming him somewhat. His hand hovered over his decanter of brandy. He could almost hear Clarissa berating him slightly for turning to alcohol again.

"She will be fine, Your Grace," Mrs. Dawson went on, her tone soothing. But even she could not keep the fear from her voice. "She will be."

Calum still did not respond. He had no words. There was no strength in him but to simply keep himself going until he knew that Clarissa was fine. He wouldn't allow himself to listen to that dark voice in the back of his mind telling him that he'd done it again.

"Your Grace." This time, the click of the door closing behind him snapped him out of his rapidly morbid thoughts. Calum walked away from the sideboard to the window. Then back. Then back again. Mrs. Dawson's eyes felt heavy as they followed him.

"Calum, please, I need you to listen to me."

Calum stopped, turning to face her. He didn't know what she saw on his face to make her stiffen so. Anguish? Dejection? Too many things were coursing through him at once so it could be any of them. Whichever one it was had forced his respectable housekeeper to address him by name and look at him as if she was watching a dead man walking. Her lips parted but the horror and concern in her eyes must have stilled her tongue.

So he continued pacing. To the desk. To the window. To the sideboard.

"I..." Mrs. Dawson let out a harsh breath. "I am afraid to say this to you, in truth, because I do not know how you will take this information. However...I cannot hold on to it much longer." Another breath, deep and inward. "I believe that Her Grace's sudden illness is not what we think it is."

Calum didn't stop his pacing. He focused on the repetition of it. Over and over and over and over, each time delaying his eventual decline of mental state. If he lost her...

If he lost her he might truly lose himself this time.

Mrs. Dawson went on, "I know you are thinking the same thing as I, Your Grace. The similarities between Her Grace's sudden illness and...and what occurred five years ago."

Calum froze. Horrible flashbacks of Violet's death tore at him before he tucked them away and continued his pacing. It wouldn't happen again, he told himself. He clung to that thought, letting it keep him afloat.

"At the time, I found it odd," Mrs. Dawson continued. "And now, I believe that my suspicions are confirmed. Her Grace's lady maid came to me a few days ago in tears asking me to remove her as the duchess' maid. She would not tell me why, but she was so distraught that I nearly allowed it. In the end, I told her that I could not move her position if she did not have a valid reason, so as not to disturb Her Grace settling in at the manor. And then..."

Calum began to listen. His pacing slowed, his attention solely on Mrs. Dawson now.

Realizing that she had his full attention, Mrs. Dawson's voice strengthened. "I saw Sarah speaking with Mr. Huntington. I do not know what was said and I do not think they noticed me. Mr. Huntington left first and Sarah began to cry. I contemplated approaching her about it but I did not get the chance."

"What does any of this have to do with Clarissa?" Calum asked at last, stopping completely to face her.

"I did not think there was any connection until now. I have a suspicion that...that Her Grace has been poisoned, Your Grace."

Calum stiffened. He folded his arms, fixing Mrs. Dawson with an intense glare. She only raised her chin and met his glare.

"You are accusing my cousin of conspiring to kill my wife?" Calum asked slowly, his voice ice.

He would have exploded if it had been anyone else. But because it was Mrs. Dawson, because she didn't look away as she said, "Yes, that is exactly what I am saying,", he felt sharp horror instead.

"It would explain why she grew so ill so quickly, Your Grace," Mrs. Dawson explained. "And Mr. Huntington has made it no secret that he is not fond of her. He was not fond of the previous duchess as well—"

"Enough!" Calum barked. He didn't want to think about this right now. Every brain cell, every emotion, he had was focused entirely on Clarissa and her well-being, praying that she would make it out of this. He didn't have the strength to focus on this right now.

Mrs. Dawson nodded as if she understood without him having to say it aloud. "I hope that I am wrong, Your Grace. But the more I think about the signs I have missed, the more I believe that I am right. The tea, for example..."

"The tea?"

Mrs. Dawson sighed and shook her head. "I think—"

The knock on the door cut her off. Mrs. Dawson glanced at Calum before she moved to open it. The trembling maid—Sarah—came in.

"Forgive me, Your Grace." She was having a hard time meeting his eyes. She looked as if she'd been crying, her cheeks splotchy and her eyes rimmed red. "The physician is finished with his examination and wishes to—"

Calum was out the door before the words were fully out her mouth. He raced back to the bedchamber, making it there in seconds. Dr. Marsh was standing outside the room when he arrived.

"How is she?" Calum heaved.

The concern on the physician's face nearly brought him to his knees. Dr. Marsh could hardly meet his eyes.

"She is...very unwell, Your Grace," he started.

"I know that!" Calum snapped. "But is she...has she..." The words lodged in his throat.

"She is resting for now." Dr. Marsh pulled out a handkerchief, wiping his sweaty brow. He stepped back to lean heavily against the wall, fingers trembling as he tucked the handkerchief away. "But her fever has not yet broken and her symptoms...they are severe."

She was alive. Relief nearly buckled Calum's knees. He raked his fingers through his hair, leaning against the opposite wall to keep himself standing. In the corner of his eyes, he noticed Mrs. Dawson and Sarah finally caught up.

"It is too late to feel relieved, Your Grace," Dr. Marsh said. With those shaking hands, he reached into his leather bag and retrieved a small pouch. "These herbs may help break her fever. Administer them to her in tea every hour for seven days and I shall return then to check on her."

Calum didn't have the strength to reach out and take the pouch. Mrs. Dawson did so instead.

"Will she be fine then?" Calum managed to say. "If—when her fever breaks, will she be like before?"

Dr. Marsh thinned his lips. He wiped his brow with the back of his hand this time, eyes darting to Calum and then to Mrs. Dawson. He quickly looked away. "It is too soon to tell."

That wasn't what he wanted to hear. But Clarissa was alive. Right now, that was the only thing he cared about.

"Thank you, Dr. Marsh," Calum mumbled as he stumbled forward. He pushed into the room, not listening for the physician's response. The moment his eyes landed on Clarissa's still, ashen face, he could focus on nothing else.

He moved to her side and gripped her hot hand in his. He didn't dare let the tears pricking the corner of his eyes fall. Vaguely, he heard Mrs. Dawson enter and close the door behind him.

"Prepare the tea," he murmured, not taking his eyes off Clarissa's face.

"Your Grace..." He sensed her hesitation. "Perhaps we should try other medication before relying on Dr. Marsh's."

Slowly, Calum twisted to look at her. The look on her face told him exactly what she was thinking. "You believe he may be involved as well."

"It is only a suspicion, Your Grace. But—"

He turned back to his wife. "Very well. I trust you. Do not let me regret it."

A pause. And then, "I will not let you regret it, Your Grace."

"Send for the village healer. She still needs medical attention."

"Yes, Your Grace."

She left him alone. As soon as she was gone, the pessimistic thoughts buzzing in the back of his mind came rushing to the forefront, consuming him whole. He gripped Clarissa's hand tightly, pushed his tears back, and prayed.

He fell asleep by her side.

Chapter Twenty-Four

She was too hot. It felt as if she was burning alive.

Clarissa tried to say as much as her eyes fluttered open but her throat was too dry, her energy too sapped. The room moved hazily before her and the odd sounds nearby felt too far and so close at once.

"She's awake," someone said.

"She is?" came another voice, this one far more familiar. That voice made her fight the wave of exhaustion that had seized her, that was forcing her eyes closed. She heard footsteps and tried to focus on them, keeping the darkness at bay long enough to say 'Yes, I am awake, my love'.

But before he could make it to her side, the darkness claimed her again.

The next time she woke, the heat was gone completely. A cool hand laid atop her forehead. Someone was humming a calming song.

Clarissa slowly opened her eyes. The first thing she noticed was that she was in her room. The second thing was that, this time, she felt less like she was fighting the urge to fall asleep again. The third thing, which should have been the first in all honesty, was that she was not alone.

"How wonderful," came a soft yet gravelly voice. "You woke earlier than I expected. I was told you were a fighter."

The back of Clarissa's eyes pained a little as she slid them to the woman standing at her bedside. She was old—far older than Mrs. Dawson—with a wrinkled face and thick gray hair tied into a braid. She was busy grinding something with a mortar and pestle, her kind eyes flicking to Clarissa now and again.

"I'm sorry," Clarissa rasped. Her throat still felt dry but not as bad as before. "I don't..."

"I know you don't know me, dear. But I certainly know you. Everyone in the village does. The lady who cured the duke's broken heart."

She finished grinding and poured what looked like herbs into a small teacup. Then she reached for a teapot that Clarissa couldn't see and poured hot water into the cup.

"It's good that you are awake," she said. "It would have been quite the task feeding this to you while you slept. Do you think you can sit up?"

Clarissa wasn't given a chance to try on her own. The woman set the hot teacup down and gripped Clarissa's upper arm with surprising strength, helping her shift up to a sitting position.

"What happened?" Clarissa murmured.

The woman picked up the teacup. "I will leave it to the duke to tell you. He will be pleased to know you are awake. But before then, drink this. I know it is hot, but you can manage, can't you?"

Again, she did not wait for Clarissa to get her bearings. She picked up Clarissa's hand and all but forced the hot tea into her palm. Then she stood back and waited expectantly.

Clarissa took a ginger sip. It tasted like hot grass but it wasn't hard to swallow. She took another sip under the woman's watchful eye before saying, "Everyone knows me because I married the duke?"

"Because you cured the duke, is what I said," the woman corrected.

"Cured is an unusual way to put it."

"Was he not suffering from heartbreak, dear? Loss can do terrible things to one's mind. We all thought he would never get over it. But when we saw you two attend the fair, there was hope that His Grace would learn to heal."

Clarissa sipped the tea again, frowning. "I thought everyone hated him. I thought you were all afraid of him."

"His Grace and his family have been a part of this village for years. I do not know what others may think of him but the villagers and I do not hate him. We worry for him. And we worried for you when we learned what happened." She clapped her hands. "But that is enough gossiping. God knows that is not the reason I was brought here. Continue drinking, dear. I shall go fetch His Grace."

Clarissa was tempted to ask her to stay to learn more. But the mention of Calum made her nod instead.

"Keep drinking, dear," the woman urged. She offered Clarissa a soft smile before she left the room.

Clarissa continued sipping. She had no memory of what happened. A haze had settled over her thoughts, like a dense cloud that refused to clear. She recalled being upset with Calum, but for what? She'd left her room, hadn't she? She'd been marching to his study before...before something happened. She just couldn't recall what.

The door banged open and her mind emptied.

Calum stood there, breathing heavily as if he had broken into a sudden sprint. His eyes were wide, staring at her as if he was seeing a ghost. Clarissa only stared back, her heart thudding in her chest. Was he upset to see her awake? Relieved? She vaguely recalled him shouting at her, though she couldn't recall what for.

"Calum—"

He rushed to her side, the movement so sudden that it startled her into silence. "How do you feel? Are you tired? How long have you been awake?"

His hands were on her—touching her cheek, her forehead, gripping her fingers as if he was scared she might slip away from him. It was worry, she realized. Worry and relief.

"I'm fine," she said softly. "I feel better."

Calum's shoulders sagged dramatically. He bowed his head, letting out a long, slow breath. He still clung to her hand. "Thank God. I thought I might have..."

"I'm here." She could feel his underlying fear like a thick heat in the room. "I'm not going anywhere."

She leaned forward, pressing her forehead against his. Calum let out another shuddering breath. At last, he lifted his eyes to meet hers.

"How do you feel?" he asked again.

"Better. Perhaps because of this?" Clarissa held up her teacup, then set it on the bedside table. "An elderly woman gave it to me."

"She is the village healer," Calum explained. "I sent for her after you..."

"After I what?" she asked gently, realizing he was having a hard time getting the words out. "I do not remember what happened."

His brows drew slightly together. "You do not? Not anything?"

"I think we might have argued. And then perhaps I was on my way to you to argue again. I do not know what it was about."

"It was..." Calum's eyes shifted away. He was still so close, almost on the bed, and still held on so tightly to her fingers that they were soon to start cramping. "It was stupid. I feel ashamed even thinking about it."

"Tell me everything."

He did, reluctantly. Shame shadowed his eyes as he told her all about the accusations he'd thrown in her face, which led her to crying in her chambers. And then shortly after, she collapsed, bedridden with a horrible fever and shortness of breath.

"The village healer said you were clinging to life," he said. As he spoke, his voice grew quieter, more somber. "That, had I wasted a second in calling her, you might not be here right now. She fought to bring you back and you fought to come back just as valiantly. That is what she told me."

"It is not your fault, Calum," Clarissa said softly. His eyes flicked to her, surprised, and she smiled. "I know that is what you have been thinking. How long have I been sleeping?"

"Eight days."

"Goodness, you spent eight days blaming yourself, haven't you?" She smiled lightly but he did not return it. "It is not your fault, Calum. The reason I am well enough to tell you that is because of you. Because you did everything you could to help me."

"I couldn't...I couldn't let you..."

"I won't leave you. You are stuck with me, Calum."

The lightness of her tone finally broke him. Clarissa realized at that moment that he had been holding himself together this entire time. The dam on his emotions broke and everything came pouring forth.

He pulled her into his chest, holding her so tightly that her breath left her lungs. Clarissa wasted no time in embracing him back.

"I love you," he rasped.

Her heart stopped.

"I was afraid that you would leave me before I got the chance to tell you. I love you, Clarissa. With all my heart and my soul." He pulled away and though there were no tears in his eyes, the rawness of his gaze cut her just as deeply. "You helped me in ways that I can hardly put in words. Before you came into my life, my days were nothing but endless pain and darkness. You are my light. I am lost without you. And...I'm sorry. For accusing you of something you did not do. For doubting you in the first place."

Clarissa blinked back her tears. "How do you know that it was not me?" she asked softly, grateful that her voice did not crack.

"Stephen confessed to framing you." Calum's voice took on a dark note. "I confronted him about it and about Mrs. Dawson's suspicions."

"Her suspicions?"

"She believed that he might have had a hand in your sudden illness, through your maid. I spoke to your maid and she told me everything that Stephen was forcing her to do, holding her employment here as blackmail. She told me that Stephen would have found a way to terminate her if she did not do as he said."

"She cannot lose her position," Clarissa said quickly. "She is the provider for her family. Her ailing grandmother and her three younger siblings will suffer if she cannot provide for them."

Calum huffed a laugh. "I tell you that my steward might have had a hand in your illness and you are more concerned for your maid."

"I am fine now, aren't I?" Clarissa reasoned with a smile.

"And for that I will be grateful for the rest of my life." As if he needed to ground himself in the presence, he kissed the back of her hand, sending butterflies through her stomach. "In the end, she revealed what Stephen had been forcing her to do. He made her watch your every move and report back to him. And after our argument, when Mrs. Dawson sent her to fetch you some tea, she slipped in a vial of liquid he had given her."

Everything came rushing back to her at once. Clarissa remembered the nature of the argument, remembered crying until she could hardly breathe while Mrs. Dawson stroked her hair. And she distinctly recalled her last interaction with Sarah.

"She didn't want me to drink it," Clarissa said. "She told me it was cold and said she would make me another, even though she'd just brought it in. I insisted."

"It doesn't matter. It was grounds for dismissal. She should be arrested."

"She was being blackmailed."

"I knew you would say that," Calum said, shaking her head. "Which is why I left her in Mrs. Dawson's hands. I focused my attention on Stephen. When I confronted him, he confessed to the blackmail but was adamant that Sarah was alone in her plot to poison. Of course, I did not believe him."

"Where is he now?"

"In police custody. As well as Dr. Percival Marsh. He is the physician who tended to you initially. Mrs. Dawson had her suspicions that he might be involved and he was. The herbs he gave me as your medicine would have only worsened your condition."

"Did Stephen blackmail him as well?"

"I do not know. I did not care. I only want justice for what they tried to do to you." He kissed the back of her hand again, then stroked the spot with his thumb.

Clarissa tried to focus on the seriousness of his words and not his constant loving touches. It was hard. "Do you think they might have done the same thing five years ago?"

Calum's face hardened. "I have no doubt. The situation was almost identical. The only difference is that you have survived it, thank God."

"Calum, I'm so sorry." She embraced him again, eyes pricking with tears. "To think someone so close to you might have been the cause of your pain all this time. I cannot imagine what you must be feeling right now."

His large hand slid around her back, resting right at the back of her neck. He held her tightly against his body. "I feel nothing but gratitude that you are still here with me. I spent days by your side praying that you would open your eyes. To think you finally did when Mrs. Dawson forced me away."

"Perhaps her intuition spoke about that as well," Clarissa laughed.

The deep rumble of his chuckle resonated through her body. "I have a question."

"Yes," she breathed. "I forgive you. I did from the moment I opened my eyes."

He let out a shuddering breath. "I have another question."

"And I love you even more now."

He pulled slightly away, searching her eyes. "I do not deserve you."

"You deserve the world, Calum."

She kissed him, softly at first. But then he leaned into it, fingers threading through her hair. It was soft, brief but perfect. As if everything had led to this beautiful moment, where their hearts became one.

Epilogue

Three Months Later

Too much time had passed. Clarissa tried to hide how restless she was getting behind soft smiles and chipper quips. But every attempt she made to sneak out of her bedchamber only told how tired she was of being on bedrest.

It turned out that narrowly escaping death from poison was not a quick recovery. The village healer was adamant that Clarissa could not overexert herself until the poison had left her system entirely, which would take quite a while. Calum took that to mean that she had to stay in bed. Clarissa took that as limited physical activity.

But he remained adamant. He didn't want to risk her falling ill again. Even though she smiled, talked, and laughed as if all was well, he stayed by her side at nights and listened to her wheeze in her sleep. He watched her struggle to eat because she had no appetite. Though her fever did not return—which the healer said was a sign that she was recovering—Calum was still on edge and did not want to take any chances.

He knew it was only a matter of time before she grew tired of his strictness, however.

She only knocked once, and briefly, before she strode into his office. Calum set his quill pen back into the pot and leaned back in his chair as she marched over to the desk.

"I am tired of staying in my room all day," she stated firmly, crossing her arms. "And I shan't have you lock me up a day longer. I am going for a walk through the gardens and then perhaps shopping in the village and you cannot stop me."

Calum grinned as she turned and began making her way to the door. She stopped with her hand on the handle and frowned back at him.

"You will not stop me?" she asked.

"You already said that I cannot."

Her confusion deepened. At that moment, he was struck all over again by how beautiful she was. He thought it as he watched her sleep. As she read her poetry in bed. As she attempted to argue with him about their own interpretations of the village healer's orders. Right now, she looked every bit the Duchess of Thorneshire with her hair atop her head and a lovely blue morning gown clinging to her soft curves.

Clarissa smoothed the confusion from her features and nodded. "Good."

Before she could leave, he said, "But I feel inclined to inform you that you may miss the surprise if you leave."

She turned to face him. "The surprise? What surprise?"

"If I tell you the details, it will ruin it, will it not?"

Clarissa was by his side in seconds. He laughed when she perched on the edge of the desk. "Give me a hint. You have been planning a surprise this entire time without me knowing? Is that why you kept me locked away?"

"I kept you locked away for your own well-being. And I do think you may be overexerting yourself right own. The poison is still in your system."

"Goodness, if it has not killed me yet, then it will not kill me now."

Calum winced at her callous words and Clarissa quickly sobered up.

"That was meant in jest," she explained. "Though, after saying it aloud, I realise it is not very funny."

"The mere mention of your death, however jokingly, will always upset me," he said lightly. Calum took her hand and pulled her to him. She let out a small sigh as she slipped into his lap. He wrapped his arms around her.

"I'm sorry," she said softly, resting her cheek atop his head. "But I do believe it is true. Which is why I need to know what the surprise is."

"How are those two related?" he asked, chuckling.

"Do not worry about the details, just know that it is." She pulled away to look at him. "So? The surprise?"

"Patience, my love." Because he could, he leaned in to peck her on the lips. Her cheeks still colored whenever he caught her off guard like that.

"I have been nothing but patient for three months," she sighed.

Calum glanced at the grandfather clock across the room. "So

a few more minutes will be nothing."

Clarissa brightened at that. "I can wait a few minutes." She looked at his desk. "What were you doing?"

"I am still going through all the records Stephen made in my ledgers," he explained, holding in a sigh. "Five years is a long time so there is a lot to go through. And, not to my surprise, quite a few discrepancies."

"How many?"

"Too many to explain. But he has been steadily siphoning my money into his pockets ever since Violet's death. My neglect made his theft go unnoticed for a while."

"I cannot believe he has held so much resentment for you for so long."

Calum could hardly believe it either. Under police questioning, the truth finally came out. At first, Stephen had stayed quiet. But when Dr. Marsh was brought in for questioning, he broke under the pressure. He revealed that he too had been blackmailed by Stephen, which led to him being an accomplice in Violet's death and the attempt on Clarissa's life. And once the truth was out, Stephen must have realized he stood no chance denying it any longer. His own truth was far darker.

Stephen's vendetta against Calum—one that Calum hadn't realized existed—had begun far before Calum inherited the dukedom, with the late duke instead. Calum knew that his father had not wanted to go into business with Stephen's father, but he hadn't realized how bitter it made Stephen. That bitterness grew when Stephen's mother grew morose after their family fell into debt and all fell on Calum when he inherited the dukedom. Calum had thought it a good idea to have Stephen as his steward at the time. He hadn't known that he had been handing his cousin the knife to bury in his back.

That resentment led to Violet's death. Stephen wanted to ruin any chances of Calum having an heir. And it almost worked if Clarissa hadn't come into his life. It might have worked again if Clarissa had not been strong enough to fight the poison long enough to receive help.

Knowing that he'd lost a trusted friend and advisor had been harder than knowing he'd lost a considerable amount of his wealth to Stephen's deception. The money he could get back. The ability to trust another with his responsiblities? Not so much.

But sitting here with Clarissa wrapped around him made everything feel better again. When he was not by her side, he was in his office working on righting his wrongs over the past five years.

"Your Grace?" his butler's voice sounded on the other end of the study door. "Your guests have arrived and are waiting in the drawing room."

"Guests?" Clarissa perked up. She frowned at him. "You have guests?"

Calum gave her a cheeky grin. "Do I?"

It took a moment for it to sink in. When it did, Clarissa leapt out of his lap, but not before giving him a loud kiss on the cheek.

"I love you so much!" she squealed before racing out the door.

Calum shook his head with a grin. There was no more hope of work for today. He stood and went after her, though she was already well down the hallway by the time he left his study.

By the time the drawing room came into view, he heard squealing. Calum walked in to see Clarissa and her sister, Louisa, locked in a tight embrace.

The rest of her family was here as well. The Earl and Countess of Santbury, the Dowager Baroness of Quelshire, and her sister. The only other person that came as a surprise was his aunt. She must have heard about the invitation and decided to invite herself.

She gave him a knowing grin but was silent in the presence of the family reunion.

"Clarissa, we're so happy to see you," the earl said, approaching. He embraced Clarissa as well, then stepped back for his wife to do the same.

"Oh, I'm so happy to see all of you," Clarissa gushed. "I know that it's been so long since I have seen you and it's because—"

"There's no need to explain," Lady Santbury said gently. "His Grace has already told us all we need to know. We're just happy that you are well now."

"Well enough," Calum added from behind. "Though she may say otherwise."

Clarissa rolled her eyes but her smile did dim when she turned to face the dowager baroness. "Mother," she breathed.

At first, Lady Quelshire did nothing but look through her. But then she blinked and took a jerky step forward. Clarissa met her halfway, reaching out to seize her hands.

"Are you happy?" Lady Quelshire asked softly, but Calum still heard.

Clarissa nodded. "Deliriously so."

Tears shone in the dowager baroness' eyes. She pulled Clarissa into a tight embrace. "Good. That is all I have ever wanted."

Calum hesitated to intrude on the tender moment and clearly so did everyone else but Miss Louisa. She launched herself into the embrace as well, squealing, "Oh, Clarissa, I am so happy for you. You must tell me everything that has happened."

"Haven't I said it all in my letters?" Clarissa asked with a laugh as she pulled away. "And what I did not, I know Calum must have explained to you."

"Not enough," her sister insisted. "I want to hear it from you."

She took Clarissa's hands and led her to the nearest sofa. At that moment, Mrs. Dawson arrived with a maid in tow. They brought refreshments. Calum watched as she laid all out while Louisa peppered Clarissa with questions. He didn't miss her small smile as she left the room.

"Before you all begin," Calum said once Mrs. Dawson was gone. "I have another surprise for you."

At that, the door opened again. This time, Mrs. Dawson entered with two footmen bearing a massive square item covered with a white cloth. Clarissa was already halfway out her seat. "Calum, is that...?"

Mrs. Dawson, still wearing that small pleased smile, nodded at one of the footmen and he pulled the white cloth away.

The portrait still took Calum's breath away. Mr. Tramp had managed to capture Clarissa's likeness perfectly. He didn't care about how he looked, though he had to admit he appeared far more alive than he had in years. Clarissa was the gem of the portrait. Her soft smile, the way in which she tilted her head slightly towards Calum, the warmth in her eyes. The very picture of the Duchess of Thorneshire.

"Oh, Calum!" Clarissa flew across the room to him. "It's

beautiful."

"You're beautiful," he murmured in her ear. And had they been alone, he would have kissed her right there. Her eyes shone as if she was thinking the same thing.

Instead, he held her close, resting his arm on the small of her back as he said to the footmen, "Hang it above the mantle."

They got into action. Everyone else was commenting on how lovely they looked as a couple but Calum hardly paid them any attention. His focus was solely on his beautiful wife in his arms.

"My heart has been encased in ice, but your presence melted even the coldest of fears within me." he said without thinking, "I never thought that my life could be this beautiful again."

She looked up at him, her eyes shimmering with happy tears. "Truthfully, neither did I. But I would not want it any other way. I love you, Calum."

"I love you too." Because everyone's attention was still on the portrait, he leaned down and brushed a kiss across her temple. "And I intend to make you the happiest lady alive for the rest of our days together."

"I am hard lady to please, you know," she teased.

"And I love a challenge."

Clarissa laughed, then rested her head against his chest. Calum found himself blinking back sudden tears. It all hit him at once, at this beautiful moment. This time last year he had been so deeply depressed that he wondered how long he could deal with the suffering. Violet's memory trailed him while awake and while asleep, never allowing him to rest. But now that he'd finally laid her to rest in his heart, he had more than enough room for Clarissa. To give her the love that she deserved. To be the man she deserved.

He had been given another chance at life through her. He would not squander it.

Extended Epilogue

Five Years Later

The small village chapel could hold no more people. Chatter hung heavily in the air as everyone waited for the christening to begin. Clarissa was struck by how many people had come to show their support. She recognized many of Louisa's friends but the number of unfamiliar faces had to be connected to Louisa's husband, the Viscount of Montgomery. To think her sociable sister had found a husband who was almost as outgoing as her was surprising indeed.

Clarissa was by herself, an unusual occurrence that she took full advantage of. She didn't know where Calum had disappeared to but he would find his way back to her side soon enough. For now, Clarissa was happy to sit in her silence and listen to snippets of conversation from everyone around her.

The village they were in was nearly half a day's ride from Thorneshire Estate. Which meant they would be spending the night at Montgomery Manor. Clarissa was already looking forward to spending some intimate time with her sister like old times.

"Here you are!" Calum was suddenly by her side.

"I was here all along," she said with smile. "Have you finished making your rounds?"

"I escaped the clutches of Lord George just now," he sighed. "If given the chance, that man will talk me into an early grave."

"It seems as if he is looking for you," she laughed. Indeed, Lord George was on the tip of his toes, peering over the many heads around him in search of something—or someone.

Calum slunk in his seat. "I would love if this christening could commence so that we can be on our way."

"Patience, my love," Clarissa chided gently.

Then she spotted Mrs. Johnson, the governess, making her way to her and her smile brightened. Holding the hands of two toddlers on either side of her, she came to a stop in front of them.

"They have calmed, Your Grace," Mrs. Johnson stated.

Clarissa was already reaching for the nearest toddler while Calum scooped up the other. Emily rested her head of dark curls on

Clarissa's chest, tears still perched on the edge of her eyes. She let out a soft sigh and Clarissa knew that her adorable daughter had cried herself into exhaustion.

Her twin sister, Emmeline, looked to be in much brighter spirits. She nibbled on her thumb finger on Calum's lap and looked around the chapel as if she was trying to see what sort of trouble she could get up to.

"Thank you, Mrs. Johnson," Calum said to the governess, who nodded with a smile and took a seat next to them.

"Are you all right, my love?" Clarissa murmured to Emily. All she did was nod, clearly too tired to do anything else.

"And you, my darling?" Calum asked Emmeline. Emmeline looked at her tired sister and mimicked her by resting her head on Calum's chest as well. When Calum gently took her thumb from her mouth, Emmeline defiantly pushed it back in.

Clarissa laughed. Calum would always say that Emily and Emmeline had one soul that shared two bodies. It wasn't so obvious as it was right now.

They fell asleep just as the ceremony began. Louisa and her husband looked lovely together by the pulpit, their newborn son bundled up in the arms of the parson between them. Clarissa felt the overwhelming urge to cry many times throughout the christening. To think that she had spent so long wanting to make sure she could provide for her sister and her family. And now Louisa was happily in love and about to start a family of her own.

Calum reached for Clarissa's hand halfway through, knowing that she was going to get overemotional.

When it was over, Clarissa handed over the sleeping Emily to Mrs. Johnson while Calum kept ahold of Emmeline. He took Clarissa's hand and led the way to Louisa, his tall and commanding presence easily parting the way.

Congratulating her sister brought forth the tears Clarissa had been trying to hold at bay all along. Louisa was brought to tears as well and their husbands simply stood aside as they hugged and kissed and spoke about how excited they were to enter this new phase of their lives.

Soon enough, Louisa and the viscount were pulled away by someone else. Clarissa met Calum's eye and he immediately knew what she wanted. Together, they made their way out of the overcrowded chapel, Mrs. Johnson falling in step behind them.

"Calum, there is something I want to tell you," Clarissa said once they were outside.

He nodded. "Let me put her down first."

Clarissa watched as he followed Mrs. Johnson to their ducal carriage. Gently, he set Emmeline down next to Emily, both under the watch of their governess. Then he jogged by to his wife's side.

"Have I ever told you how much I enjoy watching you take care of your children?" Clarissa asked, sliding her hand into his.

"Now and again, but it would not hurt to hear it another time," he said with a grin.

Clarissa laughed. "I wonder how much more doting you may become if we were to have another."

"Well, between those two troublemakers, I'm sure I will have my work cut out—" He paused, frowning at her. "Wait, what are you saying?"

"I'm saying that perhaps I won't have to wonder for too long." She grinned cheekily. "Perhaps, in a matter of months, you will have your heir."

Calum's face went slack with surprise. "Clarissa, are you..."

"I am with child again," she announced with a broad smile. "And I have a feeling that this time, it will be a son."

"I could kiss you right now," he said, pulling her into his arms.

"Do it," she challenged.

He did, deeply. As if he was pouring every bit of his love and happiness into that tender moment. Clarissa felt it deep within her soul.

"I love you, Clarissa," he murmured, pressing his forehead against hers.

"I love you too, Calum." Clarissa closed her eyes. At that moment, only they existed. And no painful memories, no vengeance, no heartache would ever stand in between them again.

The End

Printed in Great Britain
by Amazon